To Oli

with my profound

Respect —

RAPACIOUS OCTOPUS

The American Deliria

BY
EUGENE H. VAN DEE

Eugene Van Dee (signature)

Bookman LLC
Publishing & Marketing

Providing Quality, Professional
Author Services
www.bookmanmarketing.com

© Copyright 2004, Eugene H. Van Dee

All Rights Reserved.

No part of this book may be reproduced, stored in a
retrieval system, or transmitted by any means,
electronic, mechanical, photocopying, recording,
or otherwise, without written permission
from the author.

ISBN: 1-59453-317-2

Eugene Van Dee's books include:

Rimsky-Korsakov etait un Cheval (in French)

Pardon my French (in French)

Sleeping Dogs and Popsicles; The Vatican versus the KGB

Spain's Catholic Atheist; Miguel de Unamuno y Jugo and his epoch

A Tale of Wonder: from the Ballerinas of the Bolshoi to the Cancan Dancers of the Moulin Rouge

CONCORDIA UNIVERSITY LIBRARY
PORTLAND, OR 97211

DEDICATION

For John Kehagias of Athens, Greece,
my best friend and the finest man I've ever met.

APHORISM

"Whatever is well said by another is mine"
Lucius Annaeus Seneca,
Roman philosopher (3BC-AD65)

CONTENTS

INTRODUCTION

There exists a core dual principle of the modern world order that aggressive attack is prohibited in international relations and that necessary and proportional force may be used in response to such an attack. This dual principle is embodied in Articles of the United Nations Charter and in virtually every modern normative statement about the use of force in international relations. Indeed, together these two principles are the most important doctrine to emerge in more than 2000 years of human thought regarding the prevention of war.

In our contemporary world of conflicting ideology and nuclear threat, no task is more important for statesmen than maintaining the integrity of this principle in both its critical and reciprocal dimensions: prohibition of aggression and the right of defense.

Today there is a fundamental threat to this core principle, a threat that has already contributed to a serious destabilization of the world order. Unless stopped, this threat could precipitate the complete collapse of any constraints on the use of force. This threat is an assault on world order by nations whose leaders believe in the use of force for the expansion of their ideology.

Americans cherish many ideological axioms about democracy. Perhaps, the most treasured is the belief that democracies do not start wars. Conscience would be, in this instance, father to casuistry and fantasy. Not only did the United States begin the war of 1812 and the War with Mexico, it also initiated two wars involving Cuba within sixty-three years. Not even the most elaborate and sophisticated exercise in disingenuousness can deny the existence of an American empire, built by wars throughout our history.

Whether or not the United States should have intervened in Cuba and other Latin American countries is a ridiculously irrelevant question because America has been intervening in Central and South America since the 1780s. Intervention has been both direct and indirect. The United States has reacted with economic weapons as well as with ships and troops.

The United States established and has enforced limits on Cuba's economic, political, and social affairs from 1898 to this very day. Cuba's inevitable trade agreement with the Soviet Union in the early 1960's was seen as erroneous proof that Cuba had become a totalitarian Communist state. That was not the case. The ideology which produced that simple arbitrary explanation of a very complex reality was crucial because it also produced the American invasion of Cuba in 1961. Ironically this latest invasion came sixty-three years to the day after the United States went to war to pacify Cuba in 1897.

Before the end of 1959, the Central Intelligence Agency (CIA) began working with counter-revolutionary groups in Cuba. This activity increased throughout 1960 and into the first months of 1961. It involved active American military support in providing air cover for the smuggling of arms to Castro's enemies. The chronology of its Cuban operations, along with a great deal of other evidence, makes it clear that it is the CIA, rather than the military, which functions as an independent variable in the formulation and conduct of American foreign policy.

The CIA has originated projects and persuaded presidents and other high officials to authorize them on the basis of information provided by their own agency. In many cases, the CIA reported the situation, made recommendations based on their own information and then often executed suggested operations using their own agents. This one organization is a self-validating civilian agency with vast areas of independent action in foreign policy. The CIA can start wars and it is capable of fomenting revolutions. They can also spend millions of dollars without the American people and their elected officials knowing a thing about it.

The American propensity to follow the self-righteous path of least resistance, which we have practiced since we won our independence, is well known in history. Furthermore, the United States has exhibited a pronounced tendency to deal with its difficulties and to exploit its opportunities through use of economic or political force.

A rudimentary listing of our wars, quasi-wars, police actions, and interventions, makes the point. We Americans have fought the following nations: various Indian tribes, England, France, Spain, Canada, Mexico, Nicaragua, Hawaii, China, Colombia, Germany; as well as, Japan, Italy, several Eastern European countries, Korea, Vietnam, Laos, Cambodia, Afghanistan, Iraq and even the Soviet Union. (This list does not count the Cold War. Woodrow Wilson invaded Russia during his Presidency.)

We have also applied massive economic force as an instrument of policy to every nation with which we have ever had significant relations.

The distinguished writer, television personality, as well as moral and religious gadfly, Malcolm Muggeridge, observed: "In the eyes of posterity, it will inevitably seem that, in safeguarding our freedom, we destroyed it; that the vast clandestine apparatus that we built up to probe our enemies' resources and intentions, only served in the end to confuse our own purposes; that in the practice of deceiving others for the good of the state, led infallibly to our deceiving ourselves; and that the vast army of intelligence personnel built up to execute these purposes, were soon caught up in the web of their own sick fantasies, with disastrous consequences to them and us."

The CIA is both the center and the primary instrument of the cult of intelligence. It engages in espionage and counter-espionage in propaganda and in disinformation. The agency has often employed psychological warfare, to the United State's adversaries as well as America's friends. While penetrating and manipulating private institutions, the CIA creates its own organizations (called "proprietress.") The Agency recruits agents and mercenaries all over the globe; it also bribes and blackmails foreign officials to carry out its most unsavory tasks. The CIA does whatever is required in order to achieve its goals. Often, it does so without any consideration of ethics or the moral consequences of its actions.

As the secret-action arm of the American foreign policy, the CIA's most potent weapon is its covert intervention in the internal affairs of countries that the U.S. government wishes to control or to influence. Members of the cult of intelligence, including our own Presidents who approve of and often actually initiate the CIA's major undertakings, have frequently lied to protect the agency. In this way they hide their own responsibility for the operations and consequences.

The Eisenhower administration lied to the American people about the CIA's involvement in the Guatemalan coup de'état in 1954. Again, that administration lied about the agency's support of the unsuccessful rebellion in Indonesia in 1958. Ike also was dishonest about Francis Gary Powers' 1960 U-2 mission. (Powers was shot down over Soviet territory after our Government vehemently denied reconnaissance flights.)

The Kennedy administration lied about the CIA's role in the abortive 1961 invasion of Cuba at the Bay of Pigs. The United State's role was only admitted after the operation failed disastrously.

The Johnson administration was dishonest about the extent of U.S. commitments in Vietnam and in Laos. The Nixon administration publicly lied about the agency's attempt to fix the 1970 Chilean election, and its role in the assassination of its President.

G.W. Bush was dishonest to the American Congress, to the United Nations, and to the current Prime Minister of Britain, Tony Blair throughout 2001 and 2002. Bush also provided false information to the American people about Iraq's weapons of mass destruction and the imperative need to invade that country. President, James Polk said the same thing about Mexico.

Adherents of the cult of intelligence, hypocrisy and deception, like secrecy, have become standard techniques for preventing public awareness of the CIA's clandestine operations and governmental accountability for them. Furthermore, these men who ask that they be regarded as honorable men, will, when caught in their own webs of deceit, even assert that the government has an inherent right to operate in a dishonest manner regarding its own citizens.

Cuba's barter deal with the Russians in 1960, which could have been easily predicted, was largely the result of three factors: First, Cuba's serious economic problems; second, America's refusal to help solve those difficulties in any manner; and, third, the obvious realization by the Soviets that they could exploit the situation. The Soviets recognized that the short-sighted American policy gave them an irresistible invitation to cultivate a sympathetic ally on the border of the United States. Their plan was to use Cuba as a base for intelligence operations. However, at that point in time the Russians decided not to openly establish Soviet bases in Cuba, despite the fact that the United States had reportedly established similar operations in such nations as Turkey along the frontiers of the Soviet Union.

Nonetheless, Cuba did not construct airfields to handle Red Air Force bombers armed with nuclear weapons. Nor did Cuba launch reconnaissance flights over the United States. The Russians were quite aware of this difference. They understood, although many Americans did not, that their link with Cuba had not changed the essential balance of power, which stood in favor of the United States. In reaction to the Castro-Soviet trade deal, President Eisenhower approved the arming and training of Cuban counter-revolutionaries both in and outside Cuba.

Another factor that fostered hostility was that the U.S. refused to sell much-needed helicopters for agricultural purposes to Cuba. Finally, in 1960, the House of Representatives passed a law prohibiting all financial assistance to Cuba. Furthermore, the law granted the President power to fix the Cuban sugar quota, which was reduced by 700,000 short tons. These moves demonstrated how rapidly and strongly America was moving to increase its pressure on Castro.

Cuba's revolutionary government made overtures to Washington hoping to discuss the deteriorating situation. Washington declined the opportunity. The die was cast. From that point the record of American-Cuban relations reads like the script for a crude burlesque featuring action-reaction, vicious-circle diplomacy.

Castro then seized the Texaco and Esso refineries, but only after they refused to process the crude petroleum that the Soviets were sending to Cuba as aid. The American note of protest was strong, inaccurate, emotional, and filled with portents of retaliation.

This was nothing new. The United States has established and enforced limits on Cuba's economic, political, and social affairs from 1898 until today. Cuba's inevitable trade deal with the Soviet Union early in 1960 did not prove that Cuba had become a totalitarian Communist state. It only proved that they were desperate for trade.

Again, the final act of this burlesque show was that sixty-three years to the day after the United States went to war to pacify Cuba in 1897, a CIA trained army of Cuban outcasts invaded at the Bay of Pigs.

This book shines a bright light and takes a long hard look at the actions of the United States government, especially the CIA, and their overt and covert actions all over the world in the nineteenth and twentieth centuries and beyond. As you will see, in nearly every corner of the globe, the United States has been a rapacious octopus, for the most part feeding itself.

The history of modern international politics is strewn with geopolitical wreckage of states that had bid for hegemony: the Hapsburg Empire under Charles V., France under Louis XIV, and Napoleon, Bonaparte, the Victorian Britain, Hitler's Germany. They all failed. Givent eh rack record of would-be hegemons, why do American political theorists and policy makers still believe the United Stats can succeed where others have failed? It is clear that when one state becomes too powerful, it threatens other states' security and induces them to form alliances to create a geopolitical counterweight to the aspiring hegemon. American's refuse to see it that way. They claim that America's "soft power" and the appeal of its democracy and human rights legitimizes its exercise of hegemonic power. This conviction is self-serving and wrong. No state can afford to base its security on trust in the good intentions of another state. Intentions are ephemeral; today's peaceful intentions may turn malevolent tomorrow. The hegemons are threatening because they have too much power and the United States is by definition hegemonic. The fear that aspiring hegemons instill in others explains in large measure why America's hope of thwarting the rise of new great power is doomed to failure.

When our founders boldly declared America's independence to the world and our purposes to the Almighty, they knew that to endure American would have to change. Change, to preserve America's ideals: "life, liberty, the pursuit of happiness". Noble words. But if we are ever to bring together the individual and social ways of pursuing happiness, we must follow Washington's and Benjamin Franklin's example, set our jaws firmly and dedicate ourselves to the public welfare, especially now when the welfare state seems as beleaguered as Monticello.

American today is a paradox of omnipotence and vulnerability. The U.S. military budget is greater than the combined budgets of the next fourteen countries. The American economy, though imperfect, is larger than the total of the next three nations. Yet, Americans face a greater risk of sudden death than ever before. This fact has fostered a psychology that makes Americans hyper-alert to dangers from abroad as well as inclined to rely on military power to escape their fears. The Bush administration's rhetoric on preventive war does not demonstrate any sober understanding of the current American predicament. Instead, it merely repeats the disastrous strategic mistakes of earlier hegemons. To quote Prussia's Otto van Bismarck: "…preventive war is like committing suicide from fear of death".

Our untimely invasion of Saddam Hussein's Iraq breached the walls separating the one billion Muslims in 40 countries and 5 continents. We already hear the gurgle-rumbling of the poisonous hot lava in the monstrous Muslim volcano preparing to "blow". A new major terrorist attack on the United States is being prepared. Inshallah, it will fail.

CHAPTER I

MEXICO

The basic form of colonial government in Mexico was instituted in 1535 with the appointment of the first Spanish viceroy, Antonio de Mendoza. A total of sixty-one viceroys ruled Mexico from 1535 to 1821. The distinguishing characteristic of that era was the exploitation of Mexico's Native Americans.

Though decreed nominally free, in actuality the Native Americans were treated little better than slaves. As part of the *encomienda* system, the Spanish nobles, priests and soldiers were granted large tracts of land and jurisdiction over all of the Native American population in what is now Mexico.

In addition, natives were also subjected to the power of the Roman Catholic Church after Augustian, Dominican, Franciscan, and Jesuit missionaries entered the country with the Spanish *conquistadores*. Before 1859, when the Church holdings were nationalized, the Church owned one-third of all property and land in Mexico. Finally, all but the nobles suffered due to the existence of rigid social classes: at the bottom were Native Americans, the Meztisos, black slaves, freed blacks, and white Mexicans. Among the white Mexicans, the highest class was the *Peninsulares*.

Peninsulares were those who were born in Spain and later sent to hold the highest colonial offices, as opposed to the *Criollos*. *Criollos were* people of pure European descent, born and raised in New Spain who were never given high

1

office and whose resentment became an influential force in the later movement towards independence.

Throughout the vice-regal system, inefficiency and corruption greatly concerned the home Spanish government. Spain's goal was to institute administrative reforms, notably in the years 1789 to 1794 under the viceroy Juan Vicente Güémes Pacheco, conde de Revillagigedo, who was considered the greatest Spanish colonial administrator.

The turmoil of Napoleonic Europe was the backdrop and inspiration for the movement toward Mexican independence from Spain. Napoleon Bonaparte occupied Spain in 1808, and imprisoned King Ferdinand VII.

With no central authority to intervene, the administrative leaders of New Spain expelled the viceroy. In 1810, Father Miguel Hidalgo y Costilla, a parish priest in Dolores, issued the *Grito de Dolores*. Thereby, calling for the end of the rule by Spanish Peninsulares, the abolition of slavery and the end of taxes imposed on Native Americans. Captured by royalist forces, Hidalgo was shot in 1811. This event ended the first of the political civil wars that were to wrack Mexico for three-quarters of a century.

The Spanish revolution of 1820 changed the character of the rebellion in Mexico. It restored the liberal Spanish constitution and emphasized representative government. This disoriented and disenfranchised the conservative leader who then subtlety tried to separate the viceroyalty from Spain. On their behalf, General Iturbide met with Vicente Guerrero the leader of a small army. The two leaders entered into an agreement called *The Plan of Iguala*.

This agreement was written to combine their efforts in the struggle for independence. Under *The Plan of Iguala*, Mexico would become an independent country, ruled as a limited monarchy; the Roman Catholic Church would be a state church; and the Spanish and the *Criollos* would be granted equal rights.

The leadership of the insurgency next fell to Jose Maria Morelos y Pavón who, like Hidalgo, called for racial and social quality, in addition to independence. Under Morelos, the rebel forces captured vast territory including the City of Acapulco. Afterward, they declared Mexican Independence at the Congress of Chilpancingo. However, Morelos suffered a major defeat in 1813 at the hands of royalist forces under Agustin de Iturbide, a *Criolo* General. As a result he was executed.

The revolution continued under Vicente Guerrero whose army eventually fragmented into small groups, often mixing politics with banditry. This evolving revolution was the first event in a long, fierce struggle between powerful classes and the liberal democrats. A great leader to emerge among the liberals was a Native American, Benito Pablo Juarez. Famous for his integrity and unswerving loyalty to democracy, Juárez spent the next twenty-five years as the principal influence in Mexican politics. He believed that the road to economic health lay in substituting capitalism for the stifling economic monopoly held by the Roman Catholic Church and landed aristocracy. Reform in Mexico was delayed when the conservatives returned to power in 1853. Many prominent liberals including Juárez were exiled. He then returned to Mexico from the United States in 1855 and became the Minister of Justice. In his new role, Juárez was responsible for the law that abolished special courts for the clergy and the military.

The Constitution of 1857 embodied a federal form of government, universal male suffrage, freedom of speech and other civil liberties. Conservative groups, supported by Spain, bitterly opposed the new constitution and in 1858, the

War of Reform devastated Mexico. Elected president in 1861, Juárez suspended payment on foreign loans. France, Britain and Spain decided to intervene jointly in order to protect their investments.

The military intervention was spearheaded by Spain and followed by French and British contingents. The prime mover in this joint action was Napoleon III. With its strategic position and economic potential, Mexico looked especially attractive to the Napoleonic imperial scheme. When the Mexican army made a stand at Puebla in 1862, Napoleon dispatched 30,000 more troops under General ÉlieFrédéric Forey. Forey then rode as Conqueror into Mexico City. Napoleon III placed Maximilian of the House of Habsburg and his wife, Carlota, daughter of the King of Belgium, on the Mexican throne. Maximilian and Carlota ruled until 1865.

Two years later, Juárez re-conquered the country. At this time, troops under General Porfirio Diaz occupied Mexico City. Maximilian surrendered and was shot. In 1877, Diaz became president. He then dominated the history of Mexico for the next thirty-five years. Diaz, like Juárez, was a poor Indian from Oaxaca of Mixtec origin. He had become an outstanding general and a national hero in the cause against French intervention. Mexico made tremendous advances in economic development under the Diaz rule.

Although many of his new initiatives were financed and managed by foreigners, Diaz still favored rich landowners. He demonstrated this favor by assigning them communal lands that belonged to Mexican Indian's discontent spread. Diaz was then forced to resign.

Francisco Indalecio Madero became president, but he too was unable to end the political and military strife. Rebel leaders Emiliano Zapata, champion of agrarianism, and

Francisco (Pancho) Villa refused to submit to presidential authority. The life of Mexican revolutionary Emiliano Zapata was the stuff of which legends are made. For his campesinos, he was "el hombre"-the man. Zapata won his people's trust with his fairness and persistent pursuit of their best interests. Whenever he entered a village, Zapata was received with church bells and fireworks. He became the intransigent of the revolution, an immaculate symbol of the emancipation of the masses.

As a humble Indian, clothed in sandals and the white cotton uniform of the Morelian peasantry, he was placed in the pantheon of modern revolutionary heroes.

Francisco Villa, known as Pancho Villa, was originally named Doroteo Arango. Upon the outbreak of the revolution of 1910-11 against Porfirio Diaz, Villa offered his services to Francisco Indalecio Madero. Francisco was of Jewish ancestry, and had become known to his liberal admirers as "incorruptible." His supporters saw him as the perfect alternative to the long oppressive reign of Diaz. During Madero's administration, Villa served under General Victoriano Huerta, who had sentenced him to death for insubordination. Spared by Madera's assassination, Villa joined the Constitutionalist Army and became amazingly popular as the invincible champion of the war against Huerta. Alongside Montezuma and Benito Juárez, Pancho Villa is the best known and most admired Mexican throughout the world.

Villa's División del Norte was the largest revolutionary army that Latin America ever produced. Even more exceptional is the fact that the U.S. administration attempted to come to terms and forge an alliance with Villa's revolutionary movement.

What is most overlooked about the man who called himself Pancho Villa is that he represented the deepest sentiments of most Mexicans. He was not a bandit, but a political figure, a patriot who stood for simple people. The masses believed in him, and the grand and "picturesque" Villa waged war in a spectacular and chivalrous way.

While Zapata fought a small-scale guerilla war, Villa led massive cavalry charges across awesome expanses of desert. He moved huge numbers of trains, artillery and troops.

After numerous revolts, López de Santa Anna, a Centralist was elected President. It was during his presidency that disputes over what is now Texas began to mount. Thirty thousand U.S. immigrants had populated that previously desolate area. Fearing that their growing numbers posed a threat, the Mexican government closed the border to further immigration.

But enough settlers had already arrived for Texas to declare themselves an independent republic. Santa Anna gathered an army to crush the revolt, meeting with initial success by totally eliminating a Texas garrison at the Alamo. Later, he was defeated by the Texan leader Sam Houston at San Jacinto. Ten years after that, disputes between U.S. citizens and Mexicans over the western boundary of Texas led the United States to declare war. A total of five separate American armies invaded Mexico. Future US President General Zachary Taylor's army proceeded from Corpus Christi, Texas and overran Monterrey, Mexico. General Wool's troops marched from San Antonio, Texas and inured Saltillo, Mexico. General Kearney's division went westward to invade New Mexico and California. Colonel Doniphan's army marched from New Mexico to Chihuahua, Mexico and then on to Saltillo. General Scott's troops landed at Vera Cruz and afterwards, moved westward to Mexico City.

Mexican Generals Santa Anna, Ampudia, and Arista rallied their troops, but they sorely lacked uniforms, food, guns, and ammunition. This tactical crisis kept them from fighting U.S. troops effectively. As a result, they lost the war.

The Mexicans were blackmailed into signing the shameful Treaty of Guadalupe Hidalgo. This drew the boundary between Mexico and the United States at the Rio Grande and the Gila River. This new border awarded the United States more than 525,000 square miles of new territory. The new land eventually became California, Arizona, Colorado, New Mexico, Nevada, Utah and Wyoming. All of this was justified by the payment of the illusory and preposterous sum of only fifteen million dollars.

At the time, a doctrine known as Manifest Destiny was at its height in the United States. This canon expressed a belief that it was the United States of America's right and destiny to occupy the entire North American continent, including all of Mexico. American expansionists believed Mexico stood in the way of this American dream. Yet, in reality, Manifest Destiny was nothing more than a facade designed to hide U.S. territorial goals. Mexican historian Orlando Martinez calls Manifest Destiny "one of the best known euphemisms for bumptious expansionism ever minted." (In the Twentieth Century Adolph Hitler called virtually the same policy Leben's Raum.)

While the ideology of Manifest Destiny was gaining support in the United States, the Mexican government was trying to remain stable and solvent long enough to counter American expansionists. From the time of Miguel Hidalgo y Costilla's grito for independence from Spain in 1809, until the American invasion in 1846, Mexico had had a rapid succession of governments, with power struggles among the Creoles. Spain abandoned Mexico and did not respond to President Itnurbide's request to appoint a prince to rule the

Mexican Empire. In fact, Spain did not officially recognize Mexico as a sovereign nation until fifteen years after its independence.

For thirty-seven years, the Mexican people suffered violent military coups, mounting national debt and increasing class stratification between the rich and the poor. The fifty military regimes that governed sporadically from 1822-47 prevented many Mexicans from developing any real sense of national identity.

The American interest in Mexican territory was becoming increasingly naked and aggressive. Future US President, Secretary of State James Buchanan recommended that U.S. territorial goals be pursued through a policy "firmness and action towards a feeble and distracted sister republic." The most dramatic period in the history of Mexican American relations is referred to by American historians as "The Mexican War." Mexico calls the same events: "The American Invasion." The Mexican American border has been described as "una herida abierta-an open wound-where the Third World grates against the First and bleeds."

In 1846, President Polk argued that "the posture of the Mexican governments leaves the United States no other alternative for defending its national security and interests, but the declaration of war by the U.S. Congress against Mexico."

"Who is James K. Polk?" derisively asked the Whigs when the 1844 Democratic Convention nominated him. The first "dark horse" in America's political history, Polk was unknown as an orator or thinker. He was considered only a secondary figure in the field of politics. That such a man, who was colorless, plodding, as well as narrow, should become President of the United States was indeed quite incredible. His range of interests was remarkably limited.

He had never read a novel or a piece of poetry in his life, much less, seen a play. Polk knew nothing of art, of music, or of nature. He knew even less about geography and could not have cared less about cultural society. When referring to Mexico, he is quoted as saying to his cabinet, "We must teach these Brownies to our East (sic) a lesson." (N.B. readers might remember that President George Bush, speaking of his grandchildren on national television, referred to them as "the little brown ones".)

As late as 1881, the historian Hermann Von Holst spoke of the aggression against Mexico as "the war of Polk the Mendacious." The most common and accurate accusations against President Polk were that he led Congress to declare war by a tissue of perversions, ambiguities and the suppression of fact. In reality, his whole policy of foreign affairs was "tortuous and sordid."

To mobilize the opinions of U.S. legislators and the public, Polk held that Mexico had "invaded our country and had caused the shedding of American blood on U.S. territory."

Critics said that Polk carried out his program with Machiavellian adroitness. Without warning the country, and without the consent of Congress, President Polk ordered Zachary Taylor to advance to the east bank of the Rio Grande. This order was a wanton and warlike invasion of territory colonized by Mexico, to which Texas had not even a shadow of legal right. The desire to absorb Mexico did not originate with that war. For more than sixty years before the conflict, American leaders were attracted to the idea of controlling the Southwest originally held by Spain and later by Mexico. In order to rationalize the land-grabbing tendencies of the Anglo-Saxons in America, the government retained propagandists to instill a number of shibboleths supporting the scheme of expansion in the minds of the public. With such catchwords as manifest destiny, protection of religious and political freedom, and the checkmating of European machinations in the New World, true to tradition, the nation's capital was again overflowing with struts, fumes, knaves, fools, and groveling sycophants and their struggles for favor and influence.

For many years following the annexation of the department of Texas to the United States, historians in various venues echoed the words of General Francisco Mejia. Mejia was the general in chief of the Mexican forces, who in his proclamation to his troops at Metamoros in 1846 declared: "The civilized world has already recognized that in that act of war all the marks of injustice, iniquity and the most scandalous violation of the rights of nations will leave an indelible stain which will forever darken the character for virtue falsely attributed to the people of the United States; and posterity will regard with horror their perfidious conduct, and the immorality of the means employed by them to carry into effect the most degrading depredation."

Another historian observed that "the right of conquest has always been a crime against humanity; but nations jealous of their dignity and reputation have endeavored at least to cover it by the splendor of arms and the prestige of victory. To the United States it has been reserved to put into practice dissimulation, fraud, and the basest treachery in order to obtain possession, in the midst of peace, the territory of another nation." The daily *El Tiempo* said: "The American government acted like a bandit who came upon a traveler."

The American novelist, columnist and political commentator, Howard Fast, quoted Count Tolstoy who in his novel, *War and Peace*, wrote that every account of a battle was a lie. Fast added: "It would be difficult to find a war woven of so many lies (as) the 1846-48 war with Mexico. After pouring through every history of the Mexican War, writing to historians and going through old newspapers, I came to the conclusion that the Mexican War was one of the dirtiest shadows on our history, a war devised to deprive Mexico of two-thirds of its territory and manipulated and controlled by one of the worst gang of rascals ever to hold power in Washington. A President of this land calls for a world empire for forcible intervention in any land that strikes his fancy, for war which could wipe out a million human souls, and the Congress listens to him and applauds him."

In 1849, the highly respected Congregational Minister William Jay had his book, *A Review of the Causes and Consequences of the Mexican War,* published in Boston. Reverend Jay, writing with all the rage and fury of a righteous minister, indicted the government of the United States, Generals Winfield Scott and Zachary Taylor, and President James K. Polk (perhaps the most deplorable President who ever sat in the White House.)

In the closing pages of his book, Jay wrote: "...we have been taught to ring bells, and illuminate our windows, when we heard of ruin and devastation and death inflicted by our troops upon a people who never injured us, who never fired a shot on our soil, and who were utterly incapable of acting on the offensive against us."

Nicolas Trist, who was appointed by Polk to negotiate the "Treaty of Peace, Boundaries and Borders," with Mexico, later commented: "Could those Mexicans have seen into my heart, they would have known that my feeling of shame as an American was far stronger than theirs could be as Mexicans...that was a thing for every right-minded American to be ashamed of, and I was ashamed of it, most cordially and intensely ashamed of it."

In the eyes of many, the proclaimed heroic deeds of sacrifice and bravery were seen by others as foul acts of murder and crime, as well as territorial conquest as a violent dismemberment and unjustified occupation. In addition, the capture of Mexico City was a calculated and premeditated plan, whose sole purpose was to bring about the violent wrenching away of Mexico's valuable lands and resources.

Some virtuous Americans of the period might have held the hope that the history of its neighbor Mexico, the endless years of bloody struggle for independence, the value and valor of leaders such as Benito Juarez, Porfirio Diaz, and other patriots and, yes, of the rebels Pancho Villa and Emiliano Zapata would hold dominion over the insane and criminal American expansionists. That was not to be. Instead, a bloody American dagger was thrust into Mexico's very soul.

Besides, who were these heroic American generals and politicians who felt absolutely no moral constraints in trampling over the rights of gallant defenders of Mexican lands? One was "Old Rough and Ready," Zachary Taylor. This hero had behind him forty years of conquest, mostly against the Indians in the Black Hawk and the Seminole Wars in Florida. Fighting native Americans, Taylor eventually advanced to the rank of major general.

The Indian Removal Act of 1830 resulted in the uprooting of entire tribes from their homelands and their forced resettlement beyond the Mississippi river. Like so much of American history, the westward movement seemed to be a story of growth and of success. Nevertheless, for the original Americans, the Indians, it was a bitter tale of contraction and defeat.

By 1850, the white man's wars and diseases had reduced the Indian population north of the Rio Grande to half of the estimated one million who had lived there two centuries earlier. Democratic administrations in the 1830s had carried out a forced removal of 85,000 Indians of the five Indian "Civilized" nations, which consisted of the Cherokee, Choctaw, Creek, Chickasaw, and Seminole. These nations covered land they had originally settled from the southeastern states to an Indian-territory set aside for them just west of Arkansas.

Several wars stemmed from the refusal of some Native Americans to accept settlement. The effort of the Sauk and Fox to return to their homeland in early 1832 resulted in the Black Hawk War in Illinois and Wisconsin. This ended with the Bad Axe Massacre, in which most of the remaining Native Americans were killed. After the Seminole Wars, only scattered groups of Native Americans remained in the eastern part of the United States.N.B. Some fifty years later, troops under the command of General Nelson A. Miles killed 370 Sioux men, women and children in the first Massacre at Wounded Knee. (The second Massacre at Wounded Knee would occur in the Twentieth Century.)

In California alone, disease, malnutrition, and liquor (derisively called firewater by white settlers) reduced the Indian population from an estimated 150,000 to a shockingly low number of 35,000 by 1860. The reservation policy sealed the fate of the original American settlers, Native Americans. It was the concept of manifest destiny that spurred white Americans and doomed red Americans.

Next, Sam Houston provided a psychological lift with his military leadership during the war of 1812. His handling of the Black Hawk War, the Second Seminole War, and the removal of the Cherokee Indians to Oklahoma Territory, earned him high marks and promotions. At the age of sixty,

Scott achieved his major claim to fame with his ambitious amphibious expedition at Veracruz, Mexico.

Sam Houston ("The Raven") was one of the most colorful and controversial figures in Texas history. He spent most of his youth in the mountains of Tennessee with the Cherokee Indians, and was even adopted by the tribe. Serving in the Creek Campaign under Andrew Jackson, he was gravely wounded at the battle of Horseshoe Bend. After recovering, he rose to the rank of first lieutenant before resigning in 1818 in order to study law.

Ten years after that, Scott was elected Governor of Tennessee. Rather than hold the office, he instead resigned and returned to live for awhile with his longtime friends the Cherokees. Subsequently, he moved to Texas. While in Texas, Scott took control of Texas forces. He defeated Mexico's Santa Anna at the Battle of San Jacinto, thus procuring Texas independence.

Soon after the annexation of Texas, President Polk ordered Taylor and his army to the Rio Grande, opposite the Mexican City of Matamoras, where Taylor's forces were intercepted by Mexican troops. This small skirmish enabled Polk to justify his policy of aggression. His leadership choices marked the beginning of the Mexican-American War, and soon he formally declared that war in May 1846.

As American troops marched into Mexico, the Mexican army released leaflets written in English to American soldiers. The leaflets encouraged the soldiers to desert: "Come to us, we will welcome you as friends with open arms, take care of your needs, and offer you more than the Yankees can provide."

Driven by shame and desperation, many U.S. troops deserted the army throughout the war. In fact, the desertion rate was the highest of any American foreign war. In total, 9,000 to 11,000 American soldiers deserted.

EUGENE H. VAN DEE

CHAPTER II

U.S. - LATIN AMERICA RELATIONS.

Foreigners and foreign powers have greatly influenced Latin American history. Mexicans refer to the U.S.A. as the "Northern Colossus." It is not surprising that throughout the hemisphere the images that Cubans, Chileans, and Central Americans have of the United States are negative. To them, North American wealth and the corporate power or CIA plots are invariably dark and larger than life. These foreboding images are projected by some of the hemisphere's most influential writers such as José Marti, José Enrique Rodó, Pablo Neruda, Miguel Angel Asturias, Carlos Fuentes, and Gabriel Garcia Márquez.

Of course, there exist other, more benign American legacies, heroes, and mythologies. For example, Fidel Castro quoted Tom Paine and Thomas Jefferson long before he invoked Lenin. (He also loves baseball.) Mexican reporters often wrote about the strong influences that the U.S. New Left had on the Zapatista leader of Chiapas Subcomandante Marcos.

No world leader has enjoyed a more enduring and popular legend than that of the American President John F. Kennedy. The intimidating Northern colossus is also known as "El Norte, a sanctuary for Latino immigrants and refugees." In short, the U.S. presence is not always derided, opinions are varied and complex. This paradoxical presence has cast a long shadow.

In seeking to understand the influence that North Americans have had on the region in the post colonial period,

Latin Americanists and a new generation of historians of U.S. foreign relations first studied foreign investment and commercial affairs. They also knew that it was necessary for them to study diplomacy, and military interventions, relying primarily on U.S. sources. As a result, their analysis reflected prevailing notions regarding the struggle between "civilization and barbarism," the challenge posed by modernization, the specter of Communist subversion, and the deforming legacy of imperialism.

Holding center stage in the 1960s and 1970s among progressive intelligentsia north and south of the Rio Grande was the "dependency theory." This theory illustrates the structural subordination of Latin America as a periphery within the capitalist world system and was held responsible for the "development of underdevelopment," which is understood primarily in economic terms.

Like its neoclassical predecessor, "modernization/ diffusionist theory," the predominantly neo-Marxian dependency school emphasized the power and influence of the "developed" world in shaping Latin America. Consequently, the two paradigms were diametrically opposed in their interpretation of whether the results were positive or negative. With theories of imperialism and dependency under attack, and the once discredited diffusionist model recycled in "neo-liberal" form, Latin Americanists and a new generation of historians of U.S. foreign relations are challenged to study the region's relationship with the United States. To accomplish this, they turned away from dichotomous political-economic models that saw only domination, resistance, exploiters and victims.

These historians suggest alternate ways of conceptualizing the role that the U.S. and other foreign actors and agencies have played in the region during the 19th and

20th centuries. In the process, they rethought the rule of such traditional avenues of diplomatic, business, and military history and international relations theory.

After the Vietnam War, the notion that the U.S. was an imperial power gained wide acceptance. Leading politicians such as Senator J. William Fulbright described the nation's foreign policy as "imperialist." New theorists of "imperialism" were apt to focus on the U.S. political, military, and economic penetration of the Latin American periphery. Secondarily, they stressed the inexorable transfer of a type of cultural compost, the so-called American way of life.

Concerned with the question of uneven power relations between the nation-states, and with the tensions created by exports of capital-to-social formations that were in a less advanced state of development, this approach presented the multifaceted connection between two distinct political entities as well as two economies. American diplomats, businessmen, and military abroad are seen as instruments of an alliance between capital and state used to conquer markets, and to tap cheap sources of raw materials. They consolidate an asymmetrical relationship of power.

The United States is currently benefiting from elite support in Latin America for its brand of economic change. If there is little trickle down effect from the market reforms, then the United States will be pressed for more development assistance and financial support. Latin Americans will then determine if the United States is a new agent for social change, or merely the old practitioner of market access and corporate profiteering.

EUGENE H. VAN DEE

CHAPTER III

CUBA

When Columbus discovered Cuba on Sunday, October 28, 1492, he was so in awe of Cuba's charm that he called it "the most beautiful land human eyes have ever seen." The Republic of Cuba consists of the largest of the islands of the West Indies, together with adjacent islands. The island nation occupies a central location between North and South America and lies on the lanes of sea travel to all countries bounded by the Caribbean Sea and the Gulf of Mexico.

For most of its history, Cuba's fertile soil and abundant sugar and tobacco production made it the wealthiest island in the Caribbean. Between 1776 and 1825, during the time that most of the colonies of North and South America acquired their independence, Cuba's Creole elites, fearing social revolution, opted to maintain their colonial bond with Spain. With that bond, they preserved as a prosperous sugar industry. Cuba replaced Colonial St. Domingue as the world's largest producer of sugar.

Between 1878 and 1895, Cuba was in a period of social and financial disintegration. Spain increased taxes to a punishing level. An increase in the production of sugar beets in the United States caused a radical fall in the price of sugar. Because sugar was Cuba's economic mainstay this price differential drove the nation into deep economic depression. The result was massive unemployment. Large numbers of workers migrated from the countryside to urban centers while thousands of professionals left the country.

The Cubans revolted in 1895 under the inspired leadership of patriot, and writer Jose Marti who had formed the Cuban Revolutionary Party. To put down the rebellion, Spain poured more than 100,000 troops into the island.

The Spanish General Valeriano Weyler y Nicolau, known as the "Butcher," confined huge numbers of peasants in concentration camps. In these camps, thousands died of disease and starvation.

The war that America waged against Spain in 1898 marked the end of Spain's colonial empire and the rise of the United States as a global military power. A number of factors contributed to the U.S. decision to go to war against Spain. These factors included American imperialism fostered under the name of *Manifest Destiny* by many prominent U.S. publishers, such as William Randolph Hearst of The New York Journal and Joseph Pulitzer of The New York World, the sinking of the U.S. warship *Maine* and, above all, the American desire to end Spanish authority throughout South America, Central America, and Mexico.

The brutality, with which Spain denied Cuban demands for a degree of local autonomy and personal liberty, aroused both sympathy and anger in the United States. Many Americans were led to believe that the United States needed to take aggressive steps, both economically and militarily in order to establish itself as a true world power. America already had a long tradition of territorial expansion. The Louisiana Purchase of 1803, vast areas confiscated from Mexico in 1848, and the defeat and removal of Native American tribes by federal troops are just a few examples. Much of the acquired land was used to open the West to farms, ranches, speculators and corporations.

By the time the 1880s arrived, American interests dominated the lucrative sugar industry in Hawaii. Angered by U.S. domination, the islanders installed a native Hawaiian, Liliuokalani, as queen. The American planters responded by arbitrarily, and unlawfully deposing, Queen Liliuokalani. In 1898, under President William McKinley, the U.S. Congress voted to annex the Hawaiian Islands. Thus Hawaii became American territory.

A year later, the Senate ratified the peace treaty with Spain which provided that Spain would cede the Philippines, Puerto Rico, and Guam to the United States, and surrender all claims to Cuba. The U.S. paid Spain $20 million. The American Secretary of State, John Hay, called it a "splendid little war."

In a few months, the United States had become a world power with an overseas empire. But the "splendid little war" was not yet complete. The Filipinos, led by Emilio Aguinaldo, declared themselves independent. Aguinaldo, in 1899, began a three-year struggle against 120,000 U.S. troops. More than twenty thousand Filipinos were killed in combat. Another 200,000 soldiers died during the insurrection due to cholera.

The intervention of the United States altered the Cuban War of Independence from a popular insurrection by Cubans to an American victory. Before American intervention, Cuban revolutionaries controlled all Cuban territory except the major ports. As 1898 ended, it was apparent that the U.S. Army controlled the entire country. Under this control, the United States denied most of the social changes that the revolutionaries had hoped to put into effect, including their efforts to establish racial and social equality.

The majority of American political leaders, seeing themselves as Gods on Olympus, opposed an independent Cuba with a racially diverse government. Cuban independence, granted by the Treaty of Paris in 1898, was only nominal as it was under U.S. occupation. The United States and Spain negotiated the treaty that decided Cuba's fate with no Cuban representative present. The treaty left the United States firmly in control of the nominally free Cuba. The United States assumed formal military possession of Cuba on January 1, 1899, and maintained constant military occupation until May 20, 1902.

The first American military governor, General John Brook, excluded Cubans from their own government. General Brook also disbanded the Cuban army before being replaced by General Leonard Wood. General Wood sought to mitigate political division, as well as supervise elections that granted Cuba its first elected president, Tomás Estrada Palma.

Nonetheless, the Americans were primarily interested in preparing the island for incorporation into the U.S. economic system. The oppressive Platt Amendment of 1901 provided the United States the right to oversee Cuba's international commitments, its economy, internal affairs, and to establish a naval station at Guantánamo Bay.

During the 1880s and 1890s, American capitalists began heavily investing in Cuba's sugar fields. The capitalists had acquired $30 million of sugar properties by 1896, with an additional $5 million in tobacco plantations. They also bought mining properties. Iron ore, manganese, and nickel mines were acquired by Bethlehem Steel and Rockefeller interests at absurdly preferential prices. Economic and political power began to concentrate in their hands, creating economic hardships for most Cubans. The elite lost their lands and the poor lost their jobs as foreign laborers from Haiti and Jamaica, imported by American companies and working for slave wages took the place of Cuban workers.

The Cubans, meanwhile, were continuing to pursue their goal of independence from Spain. Spurred by the writings of Jose Marti, they rose-up-in-arms in 1895. Three years later, the Cubans were still waging a successful, yet undecided war. Their bloody struggle for freedom won the sympathy of many Americans. President McKinley advocated "the forcible intervention of the United States to stop the war because it was our destiny to control Cuba which was a constant menace to our peace."

McKinley neglected to mention that the day before he delivered his message to Congress, he had received a cable from the American Minister in Madrid, that immediate peace in Cuba could be secured by negotiations, that a settlement could be obtained in which Spain would grant the rebel's independence, or cede the island to the United States.

In an uprising known as "revolt of the Sergeants," Fulgencio Batista Zaldivar took over the Cuban government. The year was 1933 and the U.S. Ambassador Benjamin Sumner Welles was impressed with Batista. "You're the only individual in Cuba today who represents authority," he said.

To Batista, this was an invitation to rule. For the next decade, Batista ran the country from the background and did not demand constant recognition. Most of the time, he had his way with the government, which continued a thirty-year tradition of corruption.

It seemed plain to people all over the world that Batista was a thief and a murderer. It was plain to the people of Cuba who had suffered the loss of 20,000 of their finest sons and daughters at the hands of Batista's torturers. Nevertheless, it was not plain to the U.S. ambassadors to Cuba who were the dictator's close associates. Nor was it plain to the State Department, which disregarded the pleas of eminent Cubans to halt the shipment of arms to Batista. Still, Batista was well liked by American industry.

It was during this time that Batista formed an ignominious friendship with gangster, Meyer Lansky. Their friendship lasted over three decades. Through Lansky, the mafia knew that they had a friend in Cuba. Gangster Lucky Luciano, after being deported from the United States to Italy in 1946, went to Havana traveling under a false passport.

A summit at Havana's hotel Nacional, with mobsters such as Frank Costello, Vito Genovese, Santo Trafficante, Moe Dalitz and others, confirmed Luciano's authority over the mob. This meeting coincided with Frank Sinatra's singing debut in Havana. It was in Cuba that Lansky gave permission to kill Bugsy Siegel for skimming money from the Flamingo in Las Vegas.

A Cuban election was scheduled for June 1, 1952. A public opinion poll taken three months earlier showed that of the three candidates, Fulgencio Batista was running dead last. Ten days before the election date, Batista walked into Camp Columbia, the largest military fortress in Cuba. With great arrogance he took over the armed forces. Then U.S. President Dwight D. Eisenhower formally recognized Batista's coup and the government that he formed.

Batista opened the way immediately for large scale gambling in Havana. He was responsible for reorganizing the Cuban administration so that he and his political appointees could harvest the nation's riches. Meyer Lansky became the center of the entire Cuban gambling operation. This operation later became known as the "Latin Las Vegas."

A year after Batista's coup, a small group of revolutionaries attacked the Moncada Army Barracks in Santiago. The attack, led by Fidel Castro, failed. Castro and most of the others wound up dead or in jail. With Castro in prison, the drug and gambling business returned to normal. Mafia Boss Meyer Lansky turned Havana into an international drug port.

For a price, Batista handed contracts to dozens of U.S. corporations for massive construction projects. To appease his critics, Batista held a mock election in which he was the only candidate. He won, becoming President in 1954. He was so confident of his power that a year later, he released Castro along with the remaining survivors of the Moncada attack.

With Batista's coup d'état gnawing at his conscience, a 25-year-old lawyer appeared before the Urgency Court in Havana. This expert in law submitted a brief arguing that Batista and his accomplices had violated six articles of the Code of Social Defense for which the prescribed sentence was 108 years in prison. He demanded that the judges do their duty or hang up their robes.

Who was the foolhardy, Cuban-born, Spaniard who alone had the audacity to challenge the army cutthroat Batista? His name was Fidel Alejandro Castro Ruz. Fidel's father, Angel Castro y Argiz, had immigrated to Cuba from Galicia, in northwestern Spain. Angel had prospered in the sugar trade that had long been dominated by estates of the American-owned United Fruit Company.

Fidel entered the School of Law of the University of Havana in 1945. Later, he married Mirtha Diaz Balart, a philosophy student. Fidel's courtroom encounter with Batista clearly demonstrated that he was not, as some believed, merely a hot-headed impetuous youth whose idealism had run away from his judgment. As a strong-minded figure of power, Fidel proved that he was brilliant. It did not take him long to also prove he was courageous, and learned as a scholar of distinction in law, philosophy, and history. He also proved that he was a patriot inspired by the love of his country and a passion for justice for the dispossessed. Fidel Castro was found to be a man fired with an inextinguishable and overwhelming desire to bring honor and greatness to a sovereign Cuba. During his five-hour court brief (without consulting his notes,) Fidel astounded his listeners. By presenting references to and quotations from philosophers of ancient India that had upheld the principle of active resistance to arbitrary authority; to the ancient states of Greece and Rome, which not only admitted but defended the meting-out of death to tyrants, he impressed many.

Fidel continued by quoting from John Salisbury's book, *Book of the State man, "when a prince does not govern according to law and degenerates into a tyrant, violent overthrow is legitimate and justifiable."* Another quote from *Summa Theologica* of Thomas Aquinas, who rejects the doctrine of tyrranicide, and yet upholds the thesis that tyrants should be overthrown by the people, Martin Luther proclaimed that when government degenerates into a tyranny violating the laws, the subjects are released from their obligation to obey it. An example of a different sort would be from the French writer, Francois Hotman, from the German jurist, John Althus, or from John Locke. Jean Jacques Rousseau's *Social Contract* from the American Declaration of Independence *"... whenever any Form of Government becomes destructive ...it is the Right of the peopled to alter or abolish it",* from the French Declaration of the Rights of Man", *"...when a person seizes sovereignty, he should be condemned to death by free men."*

"Honorable Magistrates," Castro concluded, "how can you justify the presence of Batista in Power, since he gained power against the will of the people and by violating the laws of the Republic through the use of treachery and force?"

When his petition for the imprisonment of Batista was rejected by the court, Fidel decided that there was only one way in which the usurper could be overthrown and an honest government put into power. His answer was Revolution. Fidel and his brother went to Mexico to continue their campaign against the Batista regime.

In 1956, Castro and an expedition of eighty-one men landed on the coast of Oriente province, Cuba. All of them were killed or captured except for Castro, Raúl Ernesto (Che) Guevara, and nine others, who retreated into the Sierra Maestra to wage guerilla warfare against Batista's forces. With the help of a growing numbers of revolutionary volunteers throughout Cuba, Castro won a string of victories over Batista's demoralized army. His force of 800 guerillas defeated the government's 30,000-man professional army. Shortly afterwards, Batista fled the country.

As the undisputed revolutionary leader, Castro became Commander in Chief of Cuba's armed forces. In 1959, he became Premier and thus, head of government. True to his word, he vastly expanded the country's social services, extending them to all classes of society on an equal basis. Educational and health services were made available free of charge. Each, and every citizen was guaranteed employment. Cuba's privately owned commerce and industry were nationalized. Sweeping land reforms were instituted and American agricultural estates became expropriated.

The American government, long accustomed to seeing Caribbean countries as dependent clients was incensed by these policies. They launched a ferocious anti-Cuban crusade that included the arbitrary severing of all diplomatic ties without negotiation. The Bay of Pigs invasion was organized and an economic blockade of the island instituted.

At the United Nations, a French diplomat remarked: "The Americans never miss the opportunity to miss an opportunity."

A few wiser Americans knew that the U.S. should have taken Cuba, a weary and blood soaked island just ninety miles off the coast of Florida, under its protective wing. America should have acted like a Big Brother, not like a Big Bully to the tiny Cuban population (only the size of the population of New York City.) Instead, the U.S. secretly equipped thousands of Cuban exiles to overthrow Castro's government. With its economy in a crisis, Cuba had nowhere to turn.

The CIA, under pressure from President Kennedy, began a range of covert activities meant to topple President Fidel Castro. Under one such plan, the CIA sprayed the air of a radio station where Castro broadcast his speeches with a chemical that would produce hallucinatory reactions similar to those caused by LSD.

Another scheme designed to contaminate Castro's cigars with a chemical that caused personality disorientation was presented as another way to get rid of Castro. A third CIA plan was to put thallium salts (a poisonous metallic chemical) in Castro's shoes. This would at first make his beard fall out then ultimately end his life.

One scheme was undoubtedly the most stupid and disgraceful in the long history of bad CIA ideas. The plan was to enlist the aid of the Mafia in killing Castro. Momo Salvatore Giancana was the prominent leader of The Mafia (and still is today) and confidant of Joseph Kennedy, the President's father. He was contacted through an intermediary selected by the Deputy Director of CIA operations, Sheffield Edwards. Edwards supplied Giancana with lethal pills containing botulinum toxin. However, this Mafiosi decided the scheme was just "too idiotic" and refused to carry out the mission.

The final CIA plot to kill Castro was truly weird. Following the Bay of Pigs fiasco, President Kennedy deputized his brother, Robert. Bobby Kennedy was to personally oversee the CIA's campaign against Castro. True to the Kennedy mystique, Bobby bypassed the CIA Director John McCone. Bobby also demanded regular progress reports from Desmond Fitz Gerald, a CIA officer who became head of the CIA Special Affairs Staff (SAS.) Gerald was charged with doing whatever he could to eliminate the Cuban leader.

The plots of Bill Harvey, Fitz Gerald's predecessor, had gone nowhere. Harvey had given his mob contact, John Rosselli, four poison capsules assuring him that they would be effective anywhere and at any time. Harvey also rented a U-Haul truck, filled it $5,000 worth of explosives and weapons, and left it in a parking lot. He handed the keys to Rosselli. However, Rosselli's Cuban agents were unable, or perhaps just unwilling to kill Castro.

The relationship between Robert Kennedy and Fitz Gerald was ambiguous. While Fitz Gerald admired Kennedy's boldness and willingness to cut through bureaucracy, Gerald also found Kennedy imperious and reckless.

Bobby was a force of nature willing to bully anyone. "He could sack a town and enjoy it," observed the Chairman of the Joint Chiefs of Staff, Maxwell Taylor. Also, according to Thomas Parrot, the Secretary of the Special Group of Senior Government officials, Bobby Kennedy was very difficult to deal with." He was arrogant. He thought that he knew the answer to everything. Bobby would sit with his tie down, chew gum and put his feet arrogantly up on the desk. His constant threat was, "if you don't do it, I'll tell my brother on you."

At the McClelland Hearings in 1959, Robert Kennedy, the chief counsel, described Carlos Marcello as head of the underworld in the southeastern part of the United States. Still, a year later, Bobby Kennedy solicited Marcello's help with the Louisiana delegation at the Democratic Party National Convention. Marcello turned him down, saying he was already committed to Lyndon Johnson.

Bobby Kennedy, who could never accept a refusal from anyone, promised to get even. When the Kennedys won the White House in 1960, Bobby Kennedy, now attorney general, moved quickly to expedite deportation proceedings that had hung over Marcello since the 1950 Kefauver Committee hearings.

Marcello was one of the toughest family bosses in the United States. New Orleans and Louisiana were ruled by the Marcello organization as if they were independent nation-states. Few fellow mafiosi would venture into Louisiana without first getting permission to do so.

Marcello was born Calagero Menacore in Tunis, North Africa, in 1910 of Sicilian parents and brought to the United States by his immigrant parents as an infant. He was just 20 years old when first arrested; the charge was bank robbery but it was dismissed. Over the years he was charged with illegal gambling, drug trafficking, extortion, income tax evasion—none of which led to his imprisonment. Clearly, the crime family enjoyed a cozy relationship with many local and state officials in Louisiana.

Marcello took up the reins of the New Orleans crime family when its boss, Sam Carrole, was imprisoned. He assumed command and helped to arrange the shipment of slot machines from New york city into New Orleans, after negotiating with powerful gangsters in New York such as Charles "Lucky" Luciano, Meyer Lansky, and Frank Costello. The political figure behind the invitation to the New York underworld to send gambling equipment was Senator Huey "Kingfish" Long. Marcello deftly arranged for the New York crime syndicate to supply the capital, while Long furnished the political protection. The New Orleans Cosa Nostra crime family supervised operations, drawing off a good percentage of the profits.

Ignoring all laws, the brazen, unbelievably arrogant Robert Kennedy arranged for Marcello, who held only a dubious Guatamalan passport, to be seized by government agents, zipped off to an airport, hustled aboard A78-seat jet and deposited in Guatemala. The unhappy Guatemalan government had Marcello and his American lawyer flown to a jungle village in El Salvador where soldiers dumped the two expensively dressed men in the mountains. They were then shunted out of the country into Honduras. The most feared man in Louisiana. Slipping secretly into New Orleans he found an unjustified tax lien for more than $800,000 awaiting him. He vowed revenge against the Kennedys. Several theorists, who testified at the house hearings on the assassination, insisted he (Marcello) was directly responsible and that transcripts of the FBI wiretaps would prove that. However, the 13 FBI wiretaps showed no evidence that Marcello was involved in the shooting of Presient Kennedy. In a revealing wiretapped conversation with an unidentified caller Marcello said: "as for Robert Kennedy I ain't never hate him. I never did like him. How could I like a man that throwed me out to the dogs?"

Already in the past, Bobby's father Joseph had needed the mafia's help when Frank Costello, the New York Mafia boss had put a contract on his life for refusing to perform a number of owed favors. In a face-to-face meeting with Momo Giancana, the panicky Joe Kennedy blurted out, "If my son is elected President of the United States, he'll be your man. He won't refuse you ever. You have my word."

Within the week, Giancana talked to Costello. With Joe Kennedy's promise that they would have their own man in the White House, the mob called off the hit on Joe Kennedy. This was not by any means the last of the Joe Kennedy romance with the Mafiosi.

According to Tina Sinatra, Joseph Kennedy told her father (Frank) to ask Giancana to arrange for Teamsters Union support for JFK in the politically crucial West Virginia primary, and again, in Chicago during the general election. FBI wiretaps subsequently revealed large Mafia donations to the Kennedy campaign. One former federal prosecutor, G. Robert Blakey reported that the money went from Giancana to Sinatra, then to Joseph Kennedy. In return, Blakely said, "Giancana and his colleagues were convinced that the Kennedy's would do something for them." The mob took this to mean the Kennedy's would reduce FBI investigations of their activities.

Sinatra was urged by Giancana to ask the Kennedy's, especially Robert Kennedy the new Attorney General, to repay what the mafia regarded as their election debt by muzzling the Justice Department's probes into the activities of organized crime. When Bobby Kennedy formed the McClellan Committee in order to investigate mob activity, Giancana and other top mobsters were served subpoenas to appear before the committee. Giancana began having second thoughts about the Kennedy's and he began working on a defense against them.

John F. Kennedy had the reputation of being a real womanizer. Therefore, it did not take long, especially with the help of mob whoremasters and local police, both on Momo's payroll, to collect incriminating evidence. As he confessed to his brother, "I got enough evidence to ruin two political careers. I've got pictures, tape recordings, film, you name it. The American public would be real happy to see their President being serviced by three women."

On November 6, 1960, John Kennedy became President of the United States, thanks to additional help from Giancana. He controlled the unions and made them vote for Kennedy. By this time however, people in the "outfit" began to worry that Momo under pressure from the Justice Department, might break Omerta and talk. So Giancana was whacked. The order was without doubt given by another mobster, Chicago's Anthony Accardo, a former hit man for Al Capone.

Joe Kennedy's own political activities began in 1932 when he supported the Democratic presidential nomination of Franklin Delano Roosevelt. In 1938 FDR appointed Kennedy as Ambassador to England. During this sensitive period just prior to World War II, Joe Kennedy made a number of critical mistakes. He was a notoriously pro-Nazi isolationist and gave speeches expressing agreement with policies designed to appease Adolf Hitler. In dispatches to Roosevelt from London, he insisted that England could not possibly win the war with Germany and that the USA should stay out of the conflict. Without consulting the President, he also announced plans to resettle 600,000 German Jews in other parts of the world. How FDR could have appointed Joseph Kennedy, a Catholic and rabid anti British Irishman, ambassador to England remains one of the mysteries of modern diplomatic history. The choice was all the more mystifying because the President had a very low opinion of his envoy.

Earlier when he appointed Kennedy to the Securities and Exchange Commission, FDR explained to critics that while Kennedy was an inveterate fornicator, bootlegger, speculator, and crook, "It takes one to catch one". In a book edited by Amanda Smith, Joe Kennedy's grand-daughter, FDR was also quoted as saying that he (JPK) was "a very dangerous man, too dangerous to have around here." Was that the underlying reason for Kennedy's "diplomatic exile" to England? So long as Prime Minister Neville Chamberlain was pursuing appeasement Kennedy fitted in, especially since he thought Chamberlain was, next to Pope Plus XII, the greatest person he had ever met. But once war broke out Kennedy became irrelevant. When Churchill moved to the prime minister's office, Roosevelt dealt with him directly and froze Kennedy out. Kennedy came home in a huff; and for the last twenty years of his life stayed on the sidelines. He had become a super rich nobody, working through his progeny; a man highly suspicious of "Jewish conspiracies," a man of bitter hatreds, no taste, little reading, but limitless ambitions.

CHAPTER IV

CIA MEDDLING

The Soviets used the CIA's meddling in the affairs of other countries to great effect. The USA was seen by the rest of the world as imperialistic and hypocritical. If an example was needed, an ideal one was the United States overthrow of a legally elected leader, Jacobo Arbenz of Guatemala. Why? Because he nationalized 400,000 acres of idle banana plantation land owned by the U.S. United Fruit Company.

Arbenz, who had come to power in popular elections, offered the American company $600,000, the very amount that the company declared as the land's value for tax purposes. This and Arbenz's left-leaning politics were seen by Washington as cause enough to overthrow him.

If the United States actions in Guatemala were not enough, on April 17, 1961, the CIA began the invasion of Cuba at the Bay of Pigs. Had the CIA's Directorate of Operations consulted its own Directorate of Intelligence about whether the Cuban people would rise against Castro once the invasion started, they would have learned that the Cuban people would not support the invasion. Moreover, the CIA clung to the ridiculous hope that nobody would connect the invasion to the American government. That was an utterly foolish and unattainable hope. From beginning to end, the U.S. made serious mistakes that made their involvement obvious.

Then, as mentioned in Chapter III of this book, the CIA, under pressure from President Kennedy, in December 1961, began a range of other covert actions to topple and/or kill Castro.

After fumbling in Cuba, the CIA tried to control elections in Chile, this time with money. The United States spent millions of dollars to support the election of Christian Democrat, Eduardo Frei, to prevent Salvador Allende's ascension to the presidency. The US government was hostile to Allende's policies and again opposed the nationalization of American-owned companies. When Allende won the election, President Nixon sought to overthrow him through economic pressure, blocking funds from the International Monetary Fund, the World Bank and the Interamerican Development Bank. At the same time, the Nixon administration was covertly funneling a further eight million dollars to Allende's political opponents. The U.S. pressure contributed to Chile's already severe economic problems, which included high inflation and food shortages.

On September 11, 1973, President Allende was assassinated during a military coup led by General Augusto Pinochet. Eye witnesses reported that Allende was killed by an invading military force under the CIA's instructions. Official reports stated the absurd, that Allende had actually committed suicide. His family and supporters vehemently denied the possibility of suicide.

Henry Kissinger dismissed speculation among journalists and members of Congress that the CIA had precipitated Chile's economic collapse and then engineered Allende's assassination. He explained that the secret Agency "wasn't competent enough to manage an operation as difficult as the Chilean coup." Was Kissinger indulging in a bit of official lying (*plausible denial*?)

A member of his staff was quoted as saying "the CIA men were so stupid they would not be able to find their own shadow on a sunny afternoon."

Then the inimitable CIA also developed plans to assassinate Patrice Lumumba, then head of Congo (now Zaire) and was also involved in covert and paramilitary operations in Vietnam, Laos, Cambodia, Afghanistan, Angola, and Nicaragua.

In 1965-68, the CIA launched an effort (*the Phoenix Program*) in Vietnam to kill civilians that supported the Communist cause. The Program led to the deaths of 20,000 Vietnamese noncombatants. News of the killings forced many Americans to conclude that their country had committed crimes against humanity.

The CIA's troubles became even more serious when the New York Times reported, in 1974 and 1975, that the agency had violated U.S. law by spying on American citizens. These accusations claimed that the CIA opened U.S. mail, secretly placed agents in American political and religious groups and had used illegal wiretaps.

The 1975 congressional hearings also revealed that the CIA had played a significant role in coups and assassinations of political leaders in the Congo, Chile, Cuba, the Dominican Republic, Haiti, and Indonesia.

EUGENE H. VAN DEE

CHAPTER V

FIDEL ALEJANDRO CASTRO RUZ

Fidel entered the University of Havana in 1945 as an unsophisticated political novice. While at the University, he drew ideological sustenance from Cuban leftist thinkers like Julio Antonio Mella, Juan Marinello, Raúl Roa, Blas Roca, and Carlos Rafael Rodriguez. He was attracted to the Ortódoxo Party, which took a strong stand against corruption. The Ortódoxos did not blame capitalism or imperialism for many of Cuba's ills because at that time, Cubans were taught to respect and express gratitude toward the United States.

Fidel attended an international student congress in Bogota, Colombia in 1948. He witnessed the "Bogatazo" riots that occurred after the murder of liberal presidential candidate, Jorge Eliecer Gaitán. Castro concluded that the CIA had killed Gaitán because he was a popular democratic figure who advocated nationalistic reform. He realized that the United States opposed nationalism and all progressive initiatives that could have a negative effect on the profits of its corporations.

After graduating from the University with a Doctor of Law degree in 1950, Castro formed a law firm to represent the poor and politically progressive people. At this time Fidel was convinced that taking direct action was the best way to achieve political change.

Fulgencio Batista violated the Cuba's constitution and in 1952, during a coup, took control. Fidel denounced the takeover, calling Batista "a faithful dog of imperialism." In his famous five-hour long court brief against Batista, Fidel

41

argued the people's right to rebel against despotism. He stated, "Without a new conception of the state, of society, of the judicial order based on profound historical and philosophical principles, there will be no revolution that generates laws." He believed in the legitimacy of revolution and he led the abortive 1953 assault on Moncada army barracks at Santiago. He had hoped his actions would spark a national uprising against the Batista regime.

In 1953, as result of his activities at Moncada, Fidel received a fifteen-year prison sentence. He served his time on the Isle of Pines, but was released in 1955 in an amnesty, an action Batista lived to regret. While serving his sentence on Pines, Castro immersed himself in Marxist political theory. He particularly liked Marx's ability to integrate German idealism and materialism. Fidel also read Victor Hugo's study of the French revolution and its aftermath, "Napoleon le Petit." For recreation, he read the novels of Brazil's greatest fiction writer Jorge Amado. He also read the works of Fyodor Dostoevsky, Sommerset Maugham, Ivan Turgenev, Honoré de Balzac, Anatole France, Maxime Gorky, and A.J. Cronin. He familiarized himself with the writings of Immanuel Kant, Sigmund Freud, Albert Einstein, and the social legislation of Franklin Roosevelt. Fidel delved into Victor Hugo's *Les Miserables,* André Maurois's *Memoires* and Axel Munthe's *The Story of San Michele.* Munthe's book addressed the commitment to struggle against social injustice. Reading further into works of a different nature, Fidel studied exploration works by Alexander von Humbolt, and Charles Darwin. He also read Plutarch's *Parallel Lives,* as well as numerous studies in biology, engineering, genetics, finance, history, international relations, and political economy.

Castro turned his months in prison into a top-flight educational experience for himself and his associates. He organized the Abel Santamaria Ideological Academy where he and fellow inmates explored world history, philosophy and political economy. He and his associates kept abreast of world affairs, showing particular interest in the 1954 CIA sponsored overthrow of Guatemala's ten-year experiment with democracy. The Guatemala example convinced Castro that the United States would not permit nationalist reforms to occur in nations with heavy U.S. investment and that the U.S. would seek to destroy such movements using the excuse that they were inspired by the Soviet Union.

After his release from the Isle of Pines, Castro went into exile in Mexico. His goal was to prepare for his return to Cuba and the revolutionary struggle. Now Fidel studied revolutionary tactics and strategy rather than political theory.

After his arrival in Cuba, he established a guerrilla base in the Sierra Madre but hid his radical philosophy by projecting an underdog democratic social reformer image in order to win support in Cuba. Fidel also believed that his tactics would help persuade the United States to withdraw its backing of Batista.

Fidel and his compañeros added a humanitarian dimension while fighting in the Sierra. They became known as compassionate liberators and guerrilla fighters par excellence. The provisional government that took over Cuba in early 1959 technically did not include Fidel, but he was a major influence.

He gave directions from the background. He warned that his opponents would use communism as their pretext to destroy the revolution. Further, he noted that communism coexisted with capitalism in France and Italy but might not in Cuba.

Although he expressed the desire to work with and protect the rights of Communists, paradoxically, Fidel denounced as counter revolutionaries some members of Cuba's Communist Party that refused to follow his lead. While Cuba was moving from a bourgeois-democratic plan, to a socialist nation, Fidel became impatient with the pace of the Revolution. He assumed a more prominent role in accelerating change in 1959 and 1960. Afterwards, Castro enlisted the aid of the Communist Party, which he believed represented the most advanced elements of the working class. Fearing that the United States might initiate conventional or nuclear war, Cuba accepted Soviet missiles on their soil soon after the Bay of Pigs confrontation, but only to increase its security.

Castro repeatedly invoked the name Jose Marti in his speeches and essays. Both men were sons of Spanish immigrants. The two men were imprisoned on the Isle of Pines and both raised funds abroad for the struggles they led for independence. To Castro, Cuba had no greater hero than Marti, the poet, essayist and journalist. Here was another man that held a belief in the power of ideas. Marti died fighting against the Spanish in 1895 during their War of Independence, a struggle which he helped to organize. From Marti, Fidel learned how to blend humanism and *"Cubanidad"* into one revolutionary package.

Argentine physician, Ernesto "Che" Guevara helped Fidel to approach revolution theoretically. Che imparted to Fidel Lenin's belief that violence is a bestial means of settling human conflicts. Consequently, as long as society has class divisions and humans exploit humans, wars are inevitable. Che also taught Fidel that socialism is a system based as much on economics as on political consciousness. Soon, Fidel believed that Che's political thoughts would be of permanent value to a Latin American quest for change. Therefore they "brought the ideas Marxism-Leninism to their freshest, purest revolutionary expression."

Similar to the French political theorist and revolutionary thinker, Frantz Fanón, and Italian Communist Party leader, Antonio Gramsci, Fidel and Che believed that the most efficient way to build communism in Cuba was by combining the development of the material base with the development of the superstructure, rather than having them develop in successive stages. Here their thinking was in contradiction with the Soviet assumption that communist political relationships depend upon the right development of modern technological foundations.

Fidel's efforts to provide a model for revolution in Latin America were applauded by progressives at that time. However, some of the Communist parties of the region chose to reject his road to change because he had initially assigned revolutionary leadership to the guerrillas, not party cadres. Castro antagonized the members of the Communist party by denying them their self-assigned position as the vanguard of the revolution. On the other hand, Cubans preferred to think that if Marx and Lenin had never existed, Fidel would have invented communism. They say that theirs is a unique communism, not a Soviet or orthodox version. Many Cubans are proud of the fact that Castro used Marx as a guide, not as gospel; that unlike the German thinker, who set down his ideas in a ponderous fashion, Fidel put Marx's thought into a native context. He expressed his own ideas in terms easily understood by lay people. Although Castro acknowledges his debts to revolutionary precursors and especially to Che Guevara, he contends that for the most part, his political ideas result from his own reflections.

EUGENE H. VAN DEE

CHAPTER VI

BAY OF PIGS INVASION

Cuba's break with the United States, and its desire to seek economic assistance from the USSR, led to an ideological and political struggle between the nations' allied with the United States and those allied with the Soviets. The program to sabotage systematically the Castro regime had its genesis during the Eisenhower administration. Actually, it was Vice-President Richard Nixon that first suggested that the United States train Cuban exiles for an attack on Cuba.

In March 1960, at a National Security Council meeting, President Eisenhower directed the Central Intelligence Agency (CIA) to follow through on Nixon's suggestion. At the same meeting, the assassination of Castro, his brother Raul, and Che Guevara were also discussed.

Eisenhower abandoned the guerilla operations and assassination plans by November 1960. However, the head of the CIA, Allen Dulles, and the Chairman of the Joint Chiefs of Staff, General Lyman Lemnitzer, repeatedly urged paramilitary operations against Castro. One of the most influential architects of the Cold War was Walt Rostov, the chief proponent of military escalation to counter-communist revolutions. He hated revolutionary leaders such as Che Guevara, Fidel Castro and Ho Chi Minh. At a meeting of the National Security Council Staff, Rostov announced in an excited state of euphoria, "The Bolivians have executed Che Guevara; they finally got the son-of-a bitch, the last of the romantic guerillas."

47

Two days after his inauguration, Kennedy gave his approval to the invasion of Cuba at the Bay of Pigs and on April 7, 1961 the operation was launched and instantly became an absolute foreign policy fiasco. Nearly one week before the invasion, the following exchange took place at a Kennedy press conference, "Mr. President, has a decision been reached on how far this country will go in helping an anti-Castro uprising or the invasion of Cuba?" A reporter asked.

The President's reply was, "First, I want to say that there will not be, under any conditions, an intervention in Cuba by the United States Armed Forces. This government will do everything it possibly can to make certain that there are no Americans involved in any actions inside Cuba." This was technically true only because the planned invasion would be made by Cuban exiles. (What was not said was that the invaders were receiving both weapons and training from the United States.)

Both the Bay of Pigs invasion and the effort to overthrow Fidel Castro failed miserably. Fingers were pointed at the CIA. Yet, was it the President who had deceived the American people? The Kennedy acolytes blamed the CIA, the Joint Chiefs of Staff, the superiority of the Castro forces and the "Mickey Mouse" anti-Castro brigades. On that fatal morning of April 17, 1961, a total of 1,400 U.S. trained and armed "freedom fighters" (in actuality the U.S. based Cuban Expeditionary Forces (CEF)) landed at the Bahia de Cochinos (Bay of Pigs) in Cuba. Some 2,700 Cubans were involved in the operation including some 18 pilots.

When the exile troops landed, Castro took personal command of the effort to repel the invaders. The long planned action to oust Castro met a surprisingly speedy end. Cuba's revolutionary army thwarted the attack before anti-

Castro forces were able to establish a solid foothold on the island. Cuban air force pilots destroyed ships just off the beach, which were there to supply the invaders with American ammunition and communication equipment.

Cut off from this lifeline, the exile brigade struggled in vain for a few days. Before long, almost all of its members were killed or captured. The White House went into a state of shock. This failure seriously embarrassed the Kennedy administration. Blame was placed by some for not providing the invaders adequate air support. Others blamed the Kennedy Administration for allowing the attack to take place at all.

An internal secret CIA audit was prepared by CIA's Inspector, General Lyman Kirkpatrick. This report blamed the debacle on a series of mistakes made by the agency. Nonetheless, it was kept secret for thirty-six years before being released to the public in 1998. Kirkpatrick concluded that the CIA failed to provide security measures in the training and preparation of the mission; thus allowing news of the impending invasion to reach the media and more importantly Castro himself. The audit also concluded that the CIA conducted very little reliable intelligence gathering of the political situation in Cuba. Another conclusion was that the CIA wrongly predicted a wide-scale organized resistance to the Castro regime was ready to support the invaders. Of course that support, never materialized. It seemed incredible that the mightiest nation on earth, with the greatest experience in amphibious landings, could not secure a beachhead on the well-mapped territory of a neighboring island.

In the end, the Bay of Pigs fiasco was all the result of monumental stupidity and colossal bungling. From the point of view of the Cuban Revolution, the Bay of Pigs invasion could not have turned out any better. Cuba's international prestige zoomed upward. National pride soared, and with it, the Cuban's confidence in Fidel's leadership. Counterrevolution on the island received a setback from which it never recovered.

CHAPTER VII

CUBAN MISSILE CRISIS

The Cuban missile crisis began when the United States discovered that Cuba had secretly installed Soviet missiles able to carry nuclear weapons that were capable of hitting targets across most of the United States. International observers have always regarded the action as the world's closest approach to nuclear war.

Fearing that following the revolution Castro would establish a Communist regime, the U.S. applied great economic pressure. They implemented an embargo in 1960 cutting off all trade with Cuba. The ban on trade carried in American ships was later expanded to deny entry to U.S. ports to the ships of other countries en route to or from Cuba. Behind the scenes, the U.S. used diplomatic means to frustrate Cuban trade negotiations with Israel, Jordan, Iran, Greece and Japan. Castro refused to give in to the pressure. Instead, he responded by establishing closer relations with the USSR. At the time, USSR and USA were engaged in the *Cold War,* an economic military and diplomatic struggle between Communist and capitalist ideologies and nations.

By the spring of 1962, the United States began another campaign of overt and covert actions designed to weaken the Castro regime. These actions included destabilization operations and attempts to assassinate Castro himself. (As amazing and even comical as it sounds, one attempt was made to kill Castro with an exploding cigar.) Military plans for air attack and the invasion of Cuba were also prepared and leaked to the press. Therefore, it was not unreasonable for Cuban and Soviet leaders to be concerned over the intensified U.S. actions against Cuba and the possibility of an American invasion.

It was at this juncture that the Soviet leadership began to consider more far-reaching measures of military assistance to Cuba. According to the memories of Nikita Krushchev (*Kruschev Remembers,*) he first thought of stationing Soviet long-range missiles in Cuba in May 1962. "It was clear to me," wrote Kruschev, "that we may very well lose Cuba if we didn't take some decisive steps in her defense...I had the idea of installing missiles with nuclear warheads in Cuba without letting the United States find out they were there until it was too late to do anything about them." His idea was spurred by the American deployment of similar missiles near the Soviet border in Turkey.

"The Americans," he wrote, "had surrounded our country with military bases and threatened us with nuclear weapons, and now they would learn just what it feels like to have enemy missiles pointing at you; we'd be doing nothing more than giving them a little of their own medicine."

Kruschev omitted that he had given clear orders to the Soviet General in Cuba that none of the missiles would be placed on alert or in firing position. Therefore, the missiles and warhead nosecones would not be mated.U.S. intelligence confirmed that no warheads were ever even brought to the missile launch bases.

Castro, on different occasions made contradictory statements about whether the initiative was Soviet or Cuban. In an interview with the French newspaper *Le Monde*, he stated that the Soviets proposed stationing the missiles in Cuba "to strengthen the socialist camp on the world scale."

What was agitating to both Castro and to Kruschev, was not so much the threat of an actual invasion by American troops, but rather a CIA attempt to overthrow Castro by covert means.

Kruschev knew that after the *Bay of Pigs* fiasco, a CIA operation was set up under the code name Mongoose. This operation was headed by Brigadier General Edward Lansdale, the CIA officer who was given much credit for running covert operations in the Philippines and in Vietnam. The idea to destabilize Castro came from Robert Kennedy who was the driving force in this covert action using 400 Americans, 2000 Cubans, a flotilla of fast boats, and an annual budget of over $50 million.

At the time, the United States believed that the Soviet ground forces in Cuba numbered only about 20,000. (The true figure was over 42,000.) *Mongoose* was not only ineffective, but also ill-conceived enough to again make the US look foolish. One idea, recycled from past plots, was to plant some shampoo with Castro's barber containing chemicals that would cause Castro's beard to fall out and allow the poison to enter his body. In another absurd episode, the CIA succeeded in contaminating a shipload of sugar bound to the Soviet Union from Cuba. The chemical used would cause vomiting and spread distrust of Cuban sugar throughout the Soviet population.

When President Kennedy heard about this scheme, he ordered Lansdale to buy the whole shipload of sugar and to dump it into the sea. The President was now well aware both of the inadequacies of past covert operations and of the firm hold that Castro had on Cuba.

During the spring of 1962, the strains in Cuban-Soviet relations became severe. They were exacerbated by Castro's Escalante purges, which eliminated some of the more militant old-time Communists from his government. Soon afterwards, Castro sent his brother Raúl on a flying visit to

Moscow. Following his return, Castro made a speech stressing that the country was not threatened by internal uprisings, but only by an American invasion. The alarmed Soviets decided to dispatch a number of their high ranking military officers to Cuba. Among the officers was Colonel General Pavel Dankevich, Marshal of Aviation Yevgeny Ya. Savitzky, Colonel General Victor Davidkov, and Lieutenant General Stepan Grechko.

In the Meantime, the Soviets continued to deploy their giant ICBM rocket near Plesetsk (Arkhangelsk, Russia.) However, this behemoth, as the Americans later discovered, was too big and bulky to serve as a practical weapon. The Soviets eventually had to start all over again. They designed a smaller, more streamlined missile setting their ICBM program back by many months.

However, when the Kennedy administration took office, the evidence about the effectiveness of Soviet missile deployment was still inconclusive. Then, the United States launched its first successful *Corona* satellites and discovered that the missile gap was in America's favor.

For several weeks, top officials of the Kennedy inner-circle and also the intelligence community debated whether or not to tell the Soviets what they now knew. On balance, it seemed wiser to tell the truth. The U.S. Deputy Secretary of Defense Roswell Gilpatric made a public announcement. For the Soviet leadership, the signals from Gilpatric's speech and the reports of their agents on the briefings given the NATO countries were very bad news. It was not so much the fact that the Americans had military superiority because the Soviets already recognized that fact.

More alarming to them was that the Americans must have made a major intelligence breakthrough; because without it, our government would not have been able to accurately calculate the total number of deployed Soviet missiles. Nor would they have been able to pinpoint where these missiles were located, let alone have the ability to report their findings to NATO.

Thereafter, the Soviet public and diplomatic stance was a program of cover and deception. The Soviet Ambassador to the United States, Anatoly Dobrynin, informed both Robert Kennedy and Theodore Sorensen (the President's Special Assistant) that the equipment the Soviets were sending to Cuba was "defensive in nature and did not represent any threat to the security of the United States."

In a public, official statement the Soviets added: "There was no need to shift weapons for a retaliatory blow because our rockets are so powerful there was no need to search for launching sites beyond the boundaries of the Soviet Union."

Later, a four-part cable-letter from Kruschev to Kennedy likened the crisis to two men pulling on each end of a rope with a knot tied in the middle: "Mr. President, the more the two of us pull, the tighter that knot will be tied... and then it will be necessary to cut the knot, to doom the world to the catastrophe of nuclear war."

To Washington, it seemed that Kruschev had squarely faced the prospect of an escalating confrontation. Horrified at what he saw at the end of the road, he was sincerely searching for an escape. His offer was to trade Soviet missiles in Cuba for the American missiles in Turkey. The decision to withdraw the missiles required courage on the Soviet side. Kruschev deserves much of the credit, but other Soviet leaders share in it as well. The younger Soviet leaders, however, perceived his actions as weak and indecisive.

Criticized by some of the members at a meeting of the Politburo for yielding too easily to American pressure,

Kruschev barked: "I am not a Czarist officer obliged to kill myself if I fart at a masked ball. It's better to back down than go to war."

The irony is that the same problems which brought the world so near to nuclear war, later brought about the relaxation of Cold War tensions. Similarly, it was the same pressure that led the Soviets to put missiles in Cuba that later led them to take up Kennedy's proposal for a treaty banning nuclear testing.

Earlier, in this book, I wrote: "At the United Nations," a French diplomat remarked, "the Americans never miss the opportunity to miss an opportunity." I further stated, "The few wiser Americans knew that the U.S. should have taken Cuba under its protective wings. I would like to note further that had these "wiser Americans" prevailed, there would have been no Cuban missile crisis. Nor, do I believe would there have been a nuclear confrontation with the Soviets.

FAILURE TO CONSULT

On the diplomatic front, The United States committed a grave diplomatic and strategic error by ignoring Article 4 of the 1949 North Atlantic Treaty. This treaty pledged the signatories to "consult together whenever... the security of any of the Parties is threatened."

During the Cuban missile crisis when Americans and Western Europeans both faced nuclear annihilation, the Europeans were shut out of the decision-making process. The reason for this was Kennedy's Executive Committee (ExComm) dismissed any thought of sharing with the allies' decisions that could have led to nuclear destruction of North America or of Western Europe. A close reading of the language used by Kennedy and his advisers reveals the implicit judgments and unquestioned prejudices that made it easy for American leaders to assume they could and should decide questions of nuclear life and death without participation of the allies.

Words and phrases used by Kennedy, National Security Adviser McGeorge Bundy, Secretary of State Dean Rusk, and other ExComm members, described Western Europeans as "shaky, impractical, emotional and inexperienced, who had to be manipulated rather than consulted." Confident of their superior ability to manage crises-large and small, Kennedy administration officials were unwilling, or perhaps, unable, to perceive the value and possible wisdom in the views of allied leaders.

Regarding European independence, particularly in nuclear matters, Kennedy officials were not inclined to share decision-making in the crisis over the missiles in Cuba. Acting alone the Kennedy 'team' made strategic determinations for the entire alliance. Consultation remained an empty promise. President Kennedy in October 1962, unilaterally announced a blockade of Cuba and demanded that Moscow remove its missiles from that island.

These U.S. actions could have started a chain of consequences leading to a nuclear war. Yet, the Americans did not share decision-making with the allies on either issue. Instead, Kennedy kept Prime Minister Harold Macmillan, Chancellor Konrad Adenauer, de Gaulle, and other European leaders completely out of the deliberations.

The Turks had a grievance with the American President and his brother. The grievance was based upon the United States and the Soviet Union making crucial decisions about the fifteen Jupiter missiles in Turkey, proposing in a secret deal with Moscow, to swap the missiles in Turkey for the withdrawal of Soviet rockets in Cuba, all without even attempting consultations with the Ankara government. The unwillingness of Kennedy's Executive Committee to share the decision-making on this issue was motivated by the realization that some NATO allies, including the Turks, would oppose the swap. In fact, Ankara's representative to NATO had emphasized to his American Counterpart, Thomas Finletter, that Turkey regarded the Jupiters as a symbol of the alliance's determination to use atomic weapons against any Russian attack on Turkey.

Despite the ritual rhetoric about multilateral governance of the Western alliance, American leaders showed little faith in joint decision-making. Instead, they viewed allies as too fractious and too emotional to be capable of arriving at a sensible policy on a matter that threatened annihilation for Western Europe as well as for the United States.

European resentment of those who assumed themselves to be the best and the brightest helps to explain why Washington's relations with Western Europe cooled during the Kennedy years in spite of JFK's personal popularity among people in those countries.

A top British diplomat recalled that "The European governments were more unhappy with the Kennedy administration than with any other American leadership since the Second World War."

"In matters of primary importance," explained Adviser Theodore Sorensen, "Kennedy did not feel that approval by the Alliance was a condition that should in any way pressure him."

Kennedy told Secretary of State Dean Rusk, "The allies must come along or stay behind"... "we cannot accept a veto from any other power."

In the U.S. view, the chance of dissenting voices from European leaders was a sufficient reason to make the basic decisions in Washington first, and only then, inform them of the U.S. policy. U.S. leaders often tried to mitigate their treatment of individual allies as subordinates by pledging that after Western Europe united, Washington would make the new Europe an equal partner. Yet, even as they pushed for European unity, some Kennedy officials feared that a unified Europe might prove too powerful as well as too independent for the United States.

At Kennedy's request, the highly respected veteran American diplomat, David Bruce examined the problem of rising anti-Americanism in Western Europe. Bruce blamed much of it on "...the growing fear that the U.S. may want to control a strong and united Europe by smothering it in the Atlantic Community." In order to break the vicious cycle of 'European dependence and U.S. predominance,' Bruce urged Washington to treat Europe as an equal partner. Yet even this sophisticated diplomat expected the equal partner to follow America's lead and support policies determined by the United States. Bruce felt that it would be dangerous if Europe struck off on its own, seeking to play a role independent of the United States.

The determination of the U.S. to keep Western Europe within Washington's orbit, clashed with the aspirations of French President Charles de Gaulle, who sought a significant, independent voice for France in the basic decision-making of the Western alliance. For more than fifty years France had been tweaking America's nose. They refused to tow the U.S. line on subjects as diverse as NATO, Africa, the Middle East, and the Balkans. In addition, the French refused to accept the concept of what the U.S. called 'the rogue states.'

There was a growing tendency of France's leaders to criticize American unilateralism and call for a more multi-polar world, a world in which a strong Europe could provide a counterweight to the United States. Recently George W. Bush's Adviser Richard Perle voiced the American answer to that position. Bluntly, Perle said: "We don't trust the French."

THE FRENCH POSITION

Later, De Gaulle tried to unite Western Europe under French leadership to make it more independent of the United States. He insisted on building a French nuclear force that would be free from any integration with, or control from Washington. Jacques Chaban-Delmas, President of the French National Assembly argued with Kennedy that a fundamental reconstruction of the Atlantic alliance was essential. He urged the United States to recognize that Paris' ties with Bonn and with other European neighbors made France the natural channel for the coordination of policies on the Continent of Europe.

In short, De Gaulle wanted two things that the U.S. opposed: equality with Washington in the decision-making of the Western alliance and a general deference to France on Western European issues. In contrast to France, the U.S. preferred to keep most of the power itself, allowing the allies to only vent their ambitions and objections within the innocuous, multilateral frameworks of the North Atlantic Treaty Organization (NATO) and the proposed Multilateral Nuclear Force (MLF). One could argue that it matters little whether the French and the Americans disagree.

As difficult as France can be, it is one of only two allies (along with Britain) that share American values and interests. Furthermore, France has the resources, the military means, and the will to take substantial risks in the name of international security. France remains the linchpin to friendly relations with America's most vital democratic and prosperous allies. French policy is also the single most important factor in determining whether the United Nations will cooperate or compete with the United States. Americans are going to have to live with a French nation that is as proud, assertive, often infuriating, but as fundamental to world order in the twenty first century as it was in the twentieth.

Any suggestion that France and the United States always disagree would be inaccurate. From Lafayette's contribution to American independence, to the extremely close U.S.-French military cooperation in Kosovo, there have been countless examples of the two countries standing together on important, contentious issues. Examples such as the Berlin and Cuban crises in the 1950's and 1960's, the Euro missile debate in the 1980's, and Bosnia after 1994-95, just to name a few.

Still, resentment and frustration towards France are constant. In the 1940's, the driving force in Franco-American relations was General de Gaulle's deep resentment of Washington's recognition of the Vichy regime and its refusal to recognize, during wartime, the Free French as the legitimate government of France.

President Roosevelt's numerous snubs of the French in general, and De Gaulle in particular, such as excluding France from the Yalta Summit, summoning de Gaulle to meet in Casablanca (i.e. on French soil,) or planning to introduce a new French currency without French consent, intensified the estrangement. The common threads in all these insults to France were the refusal of America to take the French seriously and treat them with the respect that they deserve. They simply insist on having their positions and interests taken into account. That is not unreasonable.

Bilateral frictions erupted with America's refusal in the 1950's to support France's efforts to protect its colonial interests, despite it being clear that such global policies provided a foundation of world order and western security.

In Indochina, in 1954, the United States allowed the final French garrison at Dien Bien Phu to fall, refusing to risk American troops or even air power to save it. Two years later at Suez, the American attitude towards France was even more galling. President Eisenhower publicly opposed the French and the British intervention at Suez. He undermined our two closest allies through the manipulation of oil and currency markets. This was a deep betrayal in the eyes of the French people. Indeed, Suez proved a turning point in the way that France viewed its relationship with the United States.

To the French it meant, "never again depend on them." In Algeria—the central issue of French foreign and domestic policy from 1954 to 1962—the French received no support from Washington. Again, Washington believed that it alone decided the interests of the Western alliance, and pulling French chestnuts out of the North African fire was not part of the plan.

In 1958, General de Gaulle... determined never again to suffer the dependence on Washington that he had endured in the 1940's, created an independent French nuclear force. The force, strongly opposed by the United States, withdrew from NATO's integrated military structure. De Gaulle denounced the role of the U.S. dollar as an "exorbitant privilege" and sought to create French "national industrial champions" to overcome the dominance of U.S. based multinationals that had invested heavily in France.

The 1970's opened on a familiar note and the decade ended with disputes over detente. After 1981, new sources of friction arose. President Francois Mitterand opposed Ronald Reagan's arms build-up, refused to accept the logic of supporting "freedom fighters" in Central America, denounced the Strategic Defense Initiative, and pointed to massive U.S. budget deficits as further evidence of America's irresponsibility as a global power. An increasingly vocal critique of U.S.-led globalization and of the perils of a uni-polar world had become a central theme of French rhetoric.

It was perhaps fitting that the last major French foreign policy speeches of the century by President Jacques Chirac and Foreign Minister Vedrine in November 1999, focused on the imperative of promoting multi-polarity.

The sources of Franco-American friction over the past sixty years have been constant. France has been unwilling to play the passive junior partner in an alliance dominated by the United States. The United States has never been willing to modify its approach. Although the issues have changed—from colonial conflicts and the Cold War, to dealing with the "rogue" states and humanitarian interventions—the problem has not. Paris is still unwilling today to let Washington dictate the terms of world order.

We must not forget that for centuries before World War II, France was a major political, military and economic power. It had control not only over its own fate, but also over that of large parts of the world. France had colonial holdings in Asia, Africa, South America and the Middle East. French is still a widely used language, and French culture is appreciated around the globe. For the French, coming to terms with a fall from these heights to being a medium-sized power was painful and difficult.

Many of the clashes between the United States and France are not so much the result of differences as they are similarities. Both want to be major world powers. Both see themselves as significantly responsible for developments in various parts of the world. The United States and France both have traditions of attempting to shape the world in their own image. Both nations seem to have trouble distinguishing between what is good for them and what is good for the world as a whole. France tends to adopt a patient, laissez faire stance toward problems, seeking mainly to limit their impact. The United States impatiently searches for quick solutions.

For example, in the former Yugoslavia, the French approach, at least until 1995, was to avoid taking sides while trying to limit the damage of Serbian aggression. Conversely, the United States first insisted on avoiding involvement but after that position became unsustainable, took sides and intervened with massive military power.

In Iraq, the French and American stances were equally at variance. France did not like Saddam Hussein. However, in the absence of alternatives, it looked to ease sanctions and to live with a problem that it believed could be controlled. The United States felt it had to take action with sanctions, and air strikes to fix the problem. This was exactly the kind of gamble that the French President, Jacques Chirac, tried to dissuade George Bush from taking.

The contrasting approaches are largely the products of dissimilar histories. France's acceptance of vulnerability and its fatalism derive from centuries of living with danger, enduring invasions, and experiencing the complexities of international relations. America's "can do" attitude by contrast, results from its ignorance of history and its military and economic supremacy.

One should not expect the problems between Paris and Washington to go away anytime soon. Nonetheless, there are a few things that American leaders could do to make the relationship less tense and more productive.

First, Americans must stop treating every disagreement with France as an attack on the United States itself. A second useful principle would be to keep in mind that France would not fail to come to America's aid when it is most needed. This was true during the Cold War and it remains true today. A third suggestion is that the United States should share as much glory and credit with France and Europe as possible.

In Paris, a little bit of glory goes a long way. American gloating about its own pre-eminence and indispensability only diminishes the willingness of France and other nations to cooperate with U.S. dictates. In its relations with France, the United States should go out of its way to preclude the injection of French "theorizing" into foreign policy debates. Principles and concepts are very important to the French. It is jokingly said that if something works in practice the French want to know whether it works in theory.

FRENCH HISTORICAL ALLIANCE WITH AMERICA

In 1776, a young French aristocrat with both a great name and great possessions was fired at the young age of nineteen. He had a zeal for the American cause. "The welfare of America," he wrote to his wife, "is closely linked to the welfare of mankind."

When it became known that La Fayette intended to go fight in America, the King of France forbade it. The youth, however, chartered a ship, landed in South Carolina, and hurried on to Philadelphia. He became a major general in the American army when he was but twenty years of age. Washington praised him for his bravery. He shared Washington's victory in the attack on Trenton, but suffered defeats at Bradywine and Germantown. Later in the South, La Fayette rendered brilliant service, which made possible the final American victory at Yorktown.

Another French noble who shared with La Fayette the chief glory of the French service in America was Comte de Rochambeau. Before he left France, he made this pregnant comment on the war's outcome: "nothing without naval supremacy."

When Charles Lord Cornwallis realized that he had been beaten at Yorktown, Virginia on October 19, 1781, he ordered his second in command to deliver his sword to Comte de Rochambeau. Rochambeau was the French general who had supported George Washington in the crushing defeat of the British thanks to a powerful naval blockade by a French fleet. Responding with an elegant gesture, Rochambeau directed him to George Washington, who in turn directed him to his own second in command, Major General Benjamin Lincoln. It was the final battle of the American Revolution and the French were heroically standing with us.

Probably no other nation could have sent forth a group of aristocrats on a crusade that were so ready to fight for democratic liberty in America. Other famous French names were: Laval-Montmorency, Mirabeau, Saint-Simon, and Talleyrand. The names of the French noblemen and officers in America read like a list of medieval heroes in the Chronicles of Froissart.

The French government had sent observers to America at the time of the Stamp Act Congress in 1765. They were ready to offer positive assistance when the fighting broke out a decade later. The policy of Charles Gravier, Comte de Vergennes, the French foreign minister, was to offer covert aid to the rebels. A fictitious company was set up by the author, Pierre Augustin Caron de Beaumarchais in order to funnel military supplies to the colonists. These much-needed munitions were paid for by a secret loan from the French government.

When news of the American victory at Saratoga and the capture of the British General John Burgoyne reached Paris in December 1777, Vergennes immediately offered the Americans commercial and military alliance. A year later, the Continental Congress entered into a formal alliance with France. The French agreed to give up their claim to Canada and promised to fight until American independence had been achieved. In return, the United States opened up their trade to French merchants and agreed to support French territorial gains in the West Indies. Because of this treaty, war soon broke out between France and Britain. For the first time during the War of Independence, American success seemed possible.

At the beginning of the Revolution, the colonists knew little about the French. They shared the belief of their English cousins that they had a bad religion, starved on bad food, were addicted to bad morals and did not regard other men's wives with puritanical rigor.

The colonists were not affected by French literature because they knew nothing about it. The number of Americans that could read French was very small. The teachings of the physiocrats had no effect upon American economic thought. The political theories of Montesquieu, of Rousseau, the wit of Voltaire, the infidelities of the encyclopaedists had no influence on men since most of them did not even know these writers by name. However, the value of the French alliance was recognized by all Americans. The French soldiers made themselves very popular. The first arrivals were indeed little relished. For the most part they consisted of adventurers who came with exaggerated views of their own importance. This was no longer the case after the French government espoused the American cause, and sent over officers and soldiers from the regular army to cooperate with their American allies.

Considering the character of the average Frenchman, especially when campaigning in foreign lands, how strange to them seemed many of the customs of the colonists. Still, during the four years that the French soldiers were on our soil, there was a universal chorus of laudation over their conduct. It seemed the more meritorious when contrasted with the brutalities of the Hessians who came as enemies of the American government, but nominally, the friends of the Tories whose sympathies were still with England.

The Hessian and English soldiers plundered friend and foe with impartiality. However, the French soldiers were models of propriety. They paid for what they needed. They respected the chicken roosts, and they were polite to women. There was never a disturbance between a soldier of the French and of the American army. The propriety of French conduct deserved nothing but praise. The credit for the French men's conduct resulted largely from General Jean Baptiste Rochambeau. In the memoirs of Count Fersen, he described Rochambeau as "the only man capable of commanding us here, and of maintaining that perfect harmony which reigned between two nations so different in manners, morals and language"

In the latter years of the war, most of the gold in circulation was French gold, sent over by the French government and paid out by the French army. The farmer and the storekeeper who substituted Louis d'or for American currency naturally entertained a kindly feeling for France. When the Marquis de Chastellux was traveling in Virginia in

1782, he recorded his satisfaction on observing that most of the money staked at the cock-fights was French gold. It was found in equal abundance in other channels of trade, and the colonists viewed it with quite as much satisfaction as the marquis.

France secured the independence of her American ally but the material advantages she obtained were small recompense for a war that cost her many millions. The truth is that the French were singularly modest in their demands; they had entered the war to assist the United States, and they asked little for themselves at its close.

On the humorous side of Franco-American relations, one must certainly mention again, Charles Gravier, comte de Vergennes. He befriended Benjamin Franklin, when Congress sent Franklin to Paris as a member of the American Commission. Gravier's name should be added to those illustrious personalities responsible together with Franklin, for introducing a very particular French custom to 18th century Americans. Gravier knew of Franklin's many accomplishments; that he was a diplomat, author and that he had made many contributions to the safety and comfort of American daily life. That is why Gravier spread an entertaining "canard" about Franklin. He regaled his friends in high society with the story that while in Paris, Franklin first caught sight of what he called a wondrous, functional and awe-inspiring embellishment in Gravier's home where he was a guest.

Personally experiencing its extravagant and luxurious opulence, then fascinated by its intriguing heart like contours, Franklin described it in an article entitled: "Three great puffy rolls," subtitled "dissertation on liberty and necessity, pleasure and pain." Later, according to Gravier's story, the article also appeared in the London *Spectator*. Here, it was dutifully reported that Franklin "had become the hero of France, the symbol of enlightenment personifying the less sophisticated nobility of the New World, leading his people to freedom from the feudal past, snatching the lightning from the skies and the scepter from tyrants."

Franklin's portrait was everywhere, on objets d'art from snuffboxes to chamber pots. His society was sought after by diplomats, scientists, Freemasons, and fashionable ladies. So powerful was his influence that voguish ladies in Philadelphia of the Stuffield and the Winterbottom lineages began wearing flowered hats fashioned after the Franklin description of his French discovery.

Meantime, the French agents of prosperous Philadelphia merchants were sent scurrying through Paris in search of Franklin's gem, new or used, to send across the Atlantic. It did not take long for the French bidet to find a prominent niche there. At long last, the Americans were able to wash their feet without having to take a bath. Allah be praised.

U.S. DUPLICITY TOWARD GREAT BRITAIN:

In November 1962, the Kennedy administration excluded London from participating in the decision to cancel further development of the air-launched missile Skybolt, which President Eisenhower had promised to develop and sell to Britain. Prime Minister Macmillan prized Skybolt, which would have extended the life of Britain's V-bombers and allowed them to maintain an independent nuclear force.

Kennedy's principal advisers warned him that scuttling Skybolt would thrust upon the pro-American Macmillan a problem "so serious as to make the British government fall."

Nonetheless, Kennedy gave final approval to cancel Skybolt. The British press and many officials were outraged.

British Minister of Defense, Peter Thorneycroft stormed: "We have cancelled other projects, we have made ourselves absolutely dependent upon you." Of significance was not just Washington's exercise of superior power, but the unpardonable way in which Kennedy had failed to consult with America's closest ally.

With Skybolt scotched, the British had the choice of either building their own missile at enormous expense or giving up modern nuclear deterrent. Alternatively, they could pursue nuclear cooperation with the French; a course MacMillan knew would infuriate Washington. Another possible solution would have been for them to ask the Americans to sell to Britain the Polaris submarine-launched missile, an option that would also extend the life of Britain's independent deterrent.

MacMillan decided on the last choice and pressed Kennedy to sell the Polaris missile. However, duplicitous Kennedy officials did not wish to sell Polaris, arguing that the Skybolt cancellation would pressure London to phase out its nuclear capability, thereby setting a precedent for the post De Gaulle France and forestall nuclear ambitions in Germany.

McNamara wanted to centralize management of the West's deterrent in Washington's hands, while George Ball, Wait Rostow, Henry Owen, Robert Schaetzel, and others in the State Department argued that revitalizing the Anglo-American nuclear special relationship with the most modern strategic weapon in the U.S. arsenal would anger De Gaulle.

As a close observer noted: "They had little reason to endanger the Grand Design for the sake of fidelity to a declining ally whose defense posture of nominal independence was silly."

In the end, Kennedy and MacMillan agreed to the sale of Polaris missiles to Britain. When De Gaulle learned of this deal, he flew into a tremendously violent rage directed primarily at the British, whom he denounced for "betraying Europe."

Embittered by MacMillan's obvious preference for a nuclear special relationship with Washington rather than with Paris, the General blocked British admission to the Common Market. This also put an end to Kennedy's Grand Design.

The Kennedy administration's reluctance to share real power over decision-making reflected America's historic difficulty in treating Europeans even Britain, as equal partners.

CHAPTER VIII

NICARAGUA

The Central American country Nicaragua has a population of four million people. This tiny nation suffered constant internal conflicts and interventions by other nations, especially the United States, which shaped much of Nicaragua's history. Armed U.S. forces intervened in the 1850's when an American mercenary took over Nicaragua, and again between 1912 and 1933. U.S. marines were sent to Nicaragua several times to impose order.

Continued unrest during the 1850s set the stage for frequent United States military interventions. By 1855, a group of armed United States filibusters headed by William Walker, (a soldier of fortune, who had previously invaded Mexico,) landed in Nicaragua, reinforced by other recruits from within the United States. Walker seized Granada, which was the center of conservative power. He then assumed command of the Nicaraguan army. His call for Nicaragua's annexation by the United States as a slave state found support from United States pro-slavery forces.

Most Nicaraguans were offended by Walker's pro-slavery, pro-United States stance. Cornelius Vanderbilt who held exclusive land-and-water transit route rights across Nicaragua was determined to destroy Walker. The remainder of Central America also actively sought his demise. The struggle to expel Walker and his army proved to be long and costly. As the City of Granada burned, thousands of Central Americans lost their lives.

The final battle, called the National War, took place in the town of Rivas. The defeated Walker and his followers, escorted by U.S. marines, evacuated Rivas. They returned the American naval ships to the United States. Later, Walker made four more attempts to return to Central America. He was captured in 1860 by a British warship while trying to enter Honduras. Walker was executed by a Honduran firing squad. His activities furnished Nicaraguans with a long-lasting suspicion of United States designs upon their nation.

For more than forty years Nicaragua's government and its economy were controlled by the Somoza family, whose dictatorship was strongly backed by the United States. Marxist revolutionaries overthrew the Somozas in 1979. These revolutionaries, known as the *Sandinistas*, promised social and economic reforms. However, such efforts declined as the Sandinista government fought a devastating civil war through the 1980s against rebels (*Contras*) supported by the United States.

The United States' interest in Nicaragua, which had waned during the last half of the 1800s from isolationist sentiment following the Civil War (1861-65,) grew again during the administration of Nicaragua's President Zelaya. Angered by the American choice of Panama for the site of a canal, Zelaya made concessions to Germany and Japan for a competing canal across Nicaragua.

The United States immediately broke diplomatic relations with the Zelaya government. Soon thereafter, 400 United States marines landed on the Caribbean coast. The United States kept a contingent force in Nicaragua continually from 1912 until 1933 as a reminder of its determination to use force to keep compliant governments in power.

The Chamorro-Bryan Treaty, ratified by the American senate in 1916, transformed Nicaragua into a near United

States protectorate. Collaboration with the United States and fraudulent elections allowed the conservatives to remain in power until 1925. Fearing that a revolution in Nicaragua might result in a leftist victory, the United States sent marines again to the Caribbean coast in May 1926, ostensibly to protect American citizens and property. When violence erupted, The U.S. sent Henry Stimpson to mediate the civil war. Stimpson met with President Diaz and General José Maria Moncada, the leader of the liberal rebels. These meetings led to a peaceful solution of the crisis. The accord was known as the *Pact of Espino Negro*.

As part of this agreement, United States forces took over the country's military functions. They remained in Nicaragua to maintain order and to supervise the 1928 elections. Obviously by now, Nicaragua is familiar with both U.S. military and electoral intervention.

The U.S. military invaded Nicaragua four times during the nineteenth century. They returned in 1912 and stayed on intermittently through the next twenty years. In the 1928 elections, U.S. Marines staffed polling booths and counted the votes. It was under these "free elections," that the United States created the National Guard. The National Guard became the power base for Anastasio Somoza Garcia, founder of the Somoza family dynasty. Their intelligence and support for the United States favorably impressed the dim-witted Stimpson.

Despite its violation of the electoral process, Somoza's coup, in 1934, raised few objections in "Good Neighbor" Washington. The Somoza regime was recognized by President Roosevelt and continued to rule for forty-five years. It continued with U.S. support until it was overthrown in 1979 by the Sandinista movement begun in 1962 to oppose the regime of Anastasio Somoza Debayle. The conflict between the Somoza regime and the Nicaraguan people reached a crisis point in 1978.

The murder of Pedro Joaquin Chamorro, leader of the political opposition to Somoza, set off a national strike demanding that Somoza resign. A Sandinista commando force, headed by Eden Pastora (known as Commandante Zero) took the Nicaraguan congress hostage. In 1979, the Sandinistas launched an offensive from Costa Rica and Honduras that toppled Somoza. He then fled into exile. Afterwards, they established a junta and moved steadily to the left, eventually espousing Marxist-Leninist positions. The Sandinista dominated government was opposed by U.S.-supported guerillas known as Contras.

Relations with the United States deteriorated steadily. Ronald Reagan's administration, strongly anti-communist, was convinced that the Sandinistas were supporting guerilla forces in other Central American countries. Reagan suspended aid to Nicaragua, imposed an economic boycott, and began supplying money and arms to an opposition guerilla force.

Facing Contra attacks, Nicaragua asked for, and began receiving, military aid from Cuba and the Soviet Union. The Sandinistas candidate Daniel Ortega Saavedra won an easy victory in the elections of 1984. The United States then intervened with armed forces to dislodge the Sandinistas. Casualties from the Contra war mounted. The threat of war increased between Nicaragua and Honduras. Honduran officials allowed the contras to attack Nicaragua from bases built in their country by the United States.

Members of the U.S. Congress who opposed the Contra policy had only limited success until 1986, when the scandal known as the Iran-Contra Affair revealed that Reagan officials had already violated U.S. law in order to generate support for the Contras.

Acting against the advice of the Secretary of State George Schultz and Defense Secretary Caspar Weinberger, President Reagan undertook a covert program in an effort to obtain the release of seven American hostages held captive in Lebanon by the radical Shiite Islamic group Hezbollah. His theory was that the U.S. would sell arms to Iran, which was at war with Iraq, and the Iranian leaders would induce the kidnappers to release the hostages. (N.B. At that time, the U.S. was vigorously urging its allies to refrain from dealing with terrorists and from shipping arms to either Iraq or Iran.)

President Reagan opted to deal with the kidnappers indirectly. For the first year of this initiative, the American weapons were relayed through Israel's weapon's stockpile, with the assurance that the U.S would replenish it. This secret arrangement violated the Arms Control Act, which prohibited the transfer of U.S. arms to any recipient without the express permission of the President and notice being provided to Congress. President Reagan authorized the transfers to Iran. Still and all, he deliberately did not notify Congress. The Iran-Contra Affair was part of an interconnected series of covert operations run out of the Reagan White House by William Casey, Oliver North, Robert McFarlane and John Poindexter.

Oliver North coordinated these activities for the President. He and his colleagues inflated the price of the weapons sold to Iran and secretly diverted the excess proceeds from the United States to private Swiss bank accounts. This money was then utilized to support the Contras.

When the Senate Select Committee on Intelligence released its report on CIA assassination plots, covert operations in Chile, and CIA-FBI domestic spying activities, nearly every page contained accounts of U.S. operations in Central America and Iran. The report also contained accounts of the administration's multifaceted, multinational covert wars, the President and his men blackmailing Costa Rican politicians to support U.S. intervention in Nicaragua, bribing Contras not to engage in peace talks with the Sandinistas, laundering millions of dollars through front corporations and Swiss bank accounts conspiring in the White House to deceive the American people about the purpose of arms sales to Iran. The chief negotiator of these deals was Lieutenant Colonel Oliver North, the military aid to the National Security Council.

The sale of arms to Iran was initiated at the suggestion of the Israeli government with the dual goal of improving U.S. relations with Iran and obtaining the release of American hostages held in Lebanon by the Iranian terrorists. Profits from the multi-million arms sale were channeled to the Nicaraguan right-wing Contra guerrillas for use against the leftist Sandinista government. This too, was in direct violation of U.S. policy expressed in the so-called Bowland Amendment. Congress passed this amendment in 1984, which prohibited direct or indirect U.S. military aid to the Contras.

New details of the widening scandal emerged after a Lebanese magazine disclosed that the U.S. government had negotiated an illegal arms deal. A series of congressional investigations began. A commission headed by former U.S. Senator John Tower of Texas issued a report in 1987 castigating President Reagan and his advisers for their lack of control over the National Security Council. Reverberations concerning the ultimate responsibility for the operation continued into the 1990s.

In 1992, President George Bush, Vice President under Reagan and a man that had also been implicated but not charged in the scandal, issued pardons to many of the top officials who had been inculpated for their role in the Iran-Contra affair.

Had Congress displayed greater interest in monitoring the administration's compliance with the law regarding aid to the Contras, the Iran-Contra scandal might never have occurred. Instead, the hubris of impunity created a momentum within the national security bureaucracy to take U.S. policy further and further outside the law.

As the President, and his men, discovered the phenomenon of congressional gullibility, White House duplicity, deception, and illegal operations became just another day at the office.

EUGENE H. VAN DEE

CHAPTER IX

GUATEMALA

Guatemala has many faces. One such face would be the smiling visage of the Indian in costume seen serving guests in the gentle atmosphere of its hotels and restaurants. The cultivated upper class of Guatemalan speaking politely in excellent English is another face. It is that cultured face that would feel quite at home in the United States. Another face is that of the middle class, with its dreams of consumer goods. Sadly, all too often we see the face of the sick, undernourished lower class.

Fear and hatred, rather than a sense of common purpose unite the ten million Guatemalans. Through the cacophony of the nation's many cultures, the Indian and the Ladino, the elite few and the miserable many, the town dweller and the peasant, the civilian and the military, all share one keynote: the culture of fear. Violence, torture and death are the final arbiters of Guatemalan society, and the gods that determine behavior.

The culture of fear hails from that long dark night, which is Guatemalan history. It began with the original Spanish conquest. This conquest was one that for the Indians was a trauma from which they have not yet recovered. The lament of the Cakchiquels is as true today as it was four centuries ago, when they first bowed under the Spanish lash. The Guatemalan revolution, Jacobo Arbenz above all, with his communist supporters, challenged this culture of fear.

Between 1953 and 1954, half a million citizens (one sixth of Guatemala's population) received desperately needed land.

For the first time in the history of Guatemala, the Indians were offered land, rather than being robbed of it. The culture of fear loosened its grip over the great masses of the Guatemalan people.

The United States, however, did not approve of Arbenz. They instructed the CIA to convince Guatemala's military officers that if Guatemala did not get rid of Arbenz, the United States would. The U.S. also threatened to make them pay for their loyalty to him. In fear, the officers betrayed their President and Arbenz was overthrown. Peasants were thrown off their recently received homesteads. The culture of fear reestablished its grip over the great many and the elite strengthened their resolve never again to lose land to the Indians.

For the next thirty years, military officers beginning with Castillo Armas dominated Guatemala. Reforms that began during the revolution were reversed. With strong U.S. military and economic assistance, the governments of this period were intensely anti-communist. The military became a powerful elite class in society, with some officers gaining great wealth through corruption. With no peaceful way to seek political or social change, some Guatemalans turned to violence.

Castillo Armas was assassinated in 1957. After a period of instability, the legislature named conservative General Miguel Ydigoras Fuentes President in 1958. He soon faced a rebellion of Guatemalans who were trying to restore the progressive reforms of the period from 1944 to 1954. They were defeated, but in spite of this, some escaped and with the support of Fidel Castro. They then organized the Rebel Armed Forces, beginning the civil war.

Ydigoras allowed anti-Castro Cuban exiles supported by the United States to train in Guatemala for the ill-fated Bay of Pigs invasion of 1961. He was overthrown in 1963. General Enrique Peralta Azurdia took over the presidency and held power until 1966. During his term, right-wing terrorists known as death squads emerged. These squads murdered labor leaders and political opponents. It was during the 1970s that a series of generals again controlled the presidency. During these puppet administrations, thousands died in the continuing civil war as the government carried out a 'scorched earth' policy in which the army destroyed more than 400 indigenous villages.

Marco Vinicio Cerezo won election in 1985 as the first civilian President in fifteen years. Cerezo played a major role in bringing about the Central American Peace Accord, which contributed to the settlement of the civil war in Guatemala, as well as conflicts in Nicaragua and El Salvador.

In 1990, the United States officially cut off most of its military aid and sales of arms to Guatemala. However, the CIA secretly continued to fund the Guatemalan army with $10 million. The agency also worked to suppress reports of killings and torture by the Guatemalan military. Also, the CIA had a paid agent in Guatemala who was responsible for the 1990 torture and murder of an American innkeeper whose head was sheered off by a machete. This was not the isolated work of one overzealous agent but part of standing CIA operating procedure.

Representative Robert Torricelli of New Jersey stated in his congressional testimony, "...the agency is simply out of control and contains what can only be called a criminal element."

In El Salvador, in Guatemala, and elsewhere around the globe the 'Criminal element' was the CIA itself. It organized the death squads in these countries, financed them, equipped them, trained them, and then consulted with them on individual cases of torture and assassination. This is what the CIA does. The CIA knows it. The Pentagon knows it. The State Department knows it. The President knows it. The Congress knows it. Yet no one does anything about it. This is the agency that overthrew the democratically elected Guatemalan government of Jacobo Arbenz in 1954 because United Fruit (an American owned banana company) was worried about its plantations. Here we have an agency-that since the 1960s has worked hand-in-glove with the hemisphere's most notorious human-rights abusers. The CIA actively supported the Guatemalan military as they massacred more than 100,000 peasants and Indians and tortured even more. Here we have an agency that repeatedly violated U.S. prohibitions on aid to Guatemala. The actions of the CIA in Guatemala are a horrendous but practically unheard of scandal.

Kate Doyle, a foreign policy analyst at the National Security archive wrote that in 1953 the CIA made public a damning ten-page memorandum. This document addressed in detail how to destroy the government of Jacobo Arbenz Guzmán; Guatemala's democratically elected reformist President.

"During the past ten years," the memo began, "Guatemala has become the leading base of operations for Moscow-influenced Communism in Central America. Ruled by the powerful anti-US President Arbenz, Guatemala now represents a serious threat to hemispheric solidarity and to our security in the Caribbean area."

The memorandum further describes a 'swift, climactic military action' that included 'the neutralization of key military figures and accompanying records that also contain a list of individuals recommended for disposal.' The document describes forty years of CIA aggression in the region.

Described in graphic detail are the plans and strategies for paramilitary, diplomatic and economic warfare. It also contained the necessary provocation techniques, psychological operations, and sabotage. This memorandum not only offers an exceptionally close look at U.S. policy of that period, but also illustrates a rare view of covert CIA operations in Latin America.

In 1995, revelations about the Agency's contemporary Guatemalan operations exploded onto the public arena. A presidential panel linked members of the Guatemalan military, who were also paid agents of the CIA to crimes such as murder, torture and kidnapping. The disclosures erupted in the middle of debate in Washington on how best to reform the CIA. However, the debate between government officials, members of Congress and independent analysts focused exclusively on incremental bureaucratic changes aimed at renovating the Agency, not on changing its structure or purpose.

The CIA continued to employ legions of torturers and kidnappers to produce information concerning a part of the world where no discernable threat to national security to the United States existed. The CIA's Directorate of Plans set up clandestine projects to assassinate leading members of the Arbenz government. In a CIA 'study of Assassination,' the Agency laid out in excruciating detail its methods for murder. Sections on 'accidents,' 'drugs,' 'edge weapons,' and 'firearms' offered instructions on the most effective assassination techniques.

The 'coup' headquarters, code-named *Lincoln*, was established in Opalocka, Florida. Frank Wisner, Chief of Covert Operations reported from Opalocka directly to CIA Director Dulles. In the weeks before the coup, the CIA and its Guatemalan allies used a variety of tactics to undermine and to deceive President Arbenz and his government.

A top-secret memo dated June 1, 1954, lists proposals for stirring foreign and domestic outrage at the Arbenz Administration. Among the proposals listed were, 'simulated Guatemalan aggression against Honduras,' 'faked kidnappings of prominent Guatemalan citizens,' and 'desecration of churches with pro-Communist slogans.'

In order to frighten unfriendly government police and military officials, the CIA sent them death notices, made anonymous telephone calls in the middle of the night, and spread rumors about their personal and professional lives. In the end, the Guatemalan armed forces decided to depose President Arbenz because they feared that the United States was prepared to invade the country. In Washington, there was jubilation. The CIA scrambled to convince the White House that the operation was an unqualified and bloodless victory. They even lied to President Eisenhower about casualties suffered by rebel forces. In Guatemala, the coup left a deadly aftermath.

What the CIA had no plans for was what to do after they deposed Arbenz. The agency considered democracy an 'unrealistic' alternative for the country and envisioned a moderate authoritarian regime which would be friendly to U.S. interests. However, Guatemala's political center quickly vanished from politics into a terrorized silence. With U.S. assistance, Guatemala's military leaders developed a massive counterinsurgency campaign that left tens of thousands dead, maimed or missing. Nonetheless, the operation passed into Agency legend as an 'unblemished triumph,' and became a model for future CIA activities in the hemisphere. The art of the coup became part of the agency's standard repertoire. The list of nations afflicted by the

Agency is a long one: Cuba, Guyana, Chile, Nicaragua, and Honduras. The CIA sought to change by force or clandestine influence any regime perceived to be hostile to U.S. political, economic or national security goals. President Eisenhower signed a top-secret directive in 1960 authorizing the CIA to get rid of Castro. The result was the disaster at the Bay of Pigs. Its presumed success rested on the assumption that Castro would suffer the same loss of nerve that Arbenz did in 1954. When he did not, the Agency churned out a succession of assassination attempts against the Cuban leader. These attempts failed to kill Castro but poisoned U.S. Cuba relations indefinitely.

In Guyana, the Kennedy administration ordered a covert assault on the government of Cheddi Jagan, the freely elected Prime Minister of what was then British Guiana. Kennedy ordered the CIA to crush him and from 1961 to 1964, the Agency complied, using provocation, economic sabotage and black propaganda techniques perfected during the anti-Arbenz campaign. When the country's unions turned against him, Jagan lost his seat to a despot more receptive to U.S. interests, who then remained in power for twenty years.

In Chile, Salvador Allende's ascension to the presidency in 1970 prompted Nixon's famous order to the Director of CIA Richard Helms to 'make the economy scream.' Building on a covert program of political manipulation, propaganda, and misinformation that had been ongoing against Allende since the Kennedy administration, the CIA pursued a policy. This policy combined economic destabilization with shipments of guns and money to right-wing army officers. Thus Allende was overthrown in 1973. A violent and repressive military dictatorship replaced him and ruled for nearly two decades.

In Nicaragua, the Reagan administration's contra war against the Sandinistas was another brutal, protracted destabilization campaign. The CIA cultivated, funded and trained a counter-revolutionary force, established paramilitary bases outside the country, employed a strategy of overt and covert aggression, and exaggerated Soviet influence on the regime. Last but not least, the CIA reissued the gruesome training techniques employed in Guatemala when it circulated its 1983 murder manual. The manual advised rebel forces on the "selective use of violence" against civilians, including assassination, against "judges, magistrates, police and state security officials."

In Honduras, the United States sought the cooperation of the powerful Honduran army in its secret war against Nicaragua. The CIA played an essential role, which helped to create an army intelligence unit known as Battalion 316. Declassified documents show that the CIA trained the unit in surveillance, interrogation and torture. These methods were placed into practice in the early 1980s when Battalion 316 tortured hundreds of Honduran citizens and made hundreds more disappear.

CHAPTER X

CHILE

A republic in southwestern South America, Chile was bound on the north by Peru, on the East by Bolivia and Argentina, and the on the south and west by the Pacific Ocean.

The first European to visit the land that is now Chile was the Portuguese explorer, Ferdinand Magellan. He landed at Chiloé Island in 1520. The region was then known as *Tchili*, a Native American word meaning 'snow.'

At the time of Magellan's visit, much of southern Chile was dominated by the Araucanians, a Native American tribe remarkable for its fighting ability. Tribes occupying the northern portions of Chile had been subjugated during the 15th century by the Incas of Peru. The Spaniard Pedro de Valdivia led a second expedition into southern Chile in 1540. He succeeded in establishing several settlements including Santiago, Concepcion and Valdivia. However, the Araucanians organized an uprising killing Valdivia. The uprising was the first phase of warfare against the Spanish, and lasted nearly one hundred years. Strife continued during and after the Spanish colonial period lasting until late in the 19th century.

In 1810, Chile joined other Spanish colonies in breaking political ties with Spain by deposing the colonial governor. There was then intermittent warfare against Spanish troops dispatched from Peru. The fighting continued for more than fifteen years until 1817. At this time, nationalist rebels decisively defeated a royalist army at Chacabuco. One of the revolutionary leaders, Bernardo O'Higgins, took control of the country and ruled with dictatorial powers until 1923 when popular hostility to his regime forced his resignation. A liberal constitution was then adopted. Even so, Chile remained in turmoil until 1931 when General Joaquín Prieto became President. Ten years later, a new constitution was adopted giving enormous powers to the executive branch of the government and to the Conservative Party, which fostered policies contributing to commercial and agricultural development. During this period Chile had serious conflicts with Bolivia and Peru which were united in a confederation. In 1839 Chile invaded Peru, defeating its navy as well as the Bolivian army.

Gabriel González Videla (the Radical Party leader) won the 1946 presidential election. Videla was supported by a left wing coalition of the radical and communist parties. The coalition lasted less than six months. Under pressure from the United States, Communists were removed from the cabinet. Chile severed relations with the USSR, signed the Rio Treaty and joined the Organization of American States (OAS).

The United States then initiated a program to gain influence among Chile's army officers by training them in America and in the Canal Zone. At the same time, the CIA began a massive penetration of all sectors of Chilean society. Additionally, according to an U.S. Senate Intelligence Committee report, the agency started a number of covert actions in Chile per instructions from President Nixon. Their plan was to play a direct role in organizing a military coup.

The CIA spent millions of dollars to support the election of Christian democrat Eduardo Frei; thus preventing Salvador Allende's succession to the presidency. When Allende won the election anyway, Nixon sought to speed his overthrow through economic pressure. The policy of economic pressure articulated in memorandum 93 of the U.S. National Security Decision (NSDM) made it clear that all foreign assistance was to be stopped. The U.S. used its predominant position in international financial institutions to dry up the flow of new credit or other financial assistance to Chile.

After being installed as President, Allende quickly began to implement his campaign promises. His policies turned the country toward socialism. State control of the economy was instituted. Mineral resources and foreign banks were nationalized and land reform was accelerated. Additionally, Allende initiated a redistribution of income, price controls and raised wages. Unfortunately, the result of this initiation caused increasing economic problems. Skyrocketing prices, food shortages and political violence brought Chile to the brink of chaos. The crisis was aggravated by the United States, which continued to undermine the Allende regime. The climax came on September 11, 1973, when a military force lead by General Augusto Pinochet stormed the presidential palace and killed President Allende.

'Official reports' stated that Allende committed suicide. His family vehemently denied these reports. Eyewitnesses insisted that he was killed by the invading military assisted by CIA operatives.

Serious political analysts argue that had it not been for the position assumed by the United States, the assassination would never have taken place. They also argue Chile would have prospered economically under Allende. Political stability would have been maintained, and the Chilean military would not have moved against the Allende regime. The Colombian Gabriel Garcïa Márquez, the 1982 winner of the Nobel Prize in Literature, provided the most explicit statement of this reasoning. In an article published by

Harpers magazine in March 1974, Márquez argued that he overthrow of Allende was secretly planned in a meeting between Chilean military and Pentagon representatives in a suburb of Washington D.C. many weeks before the Chilean elections.

Other commentators described the activities of the CIA, the plotting of some American companies such as the International Telephone and Telegraph (ITT) Corporation, the activities of U.S. military personnel in Chile, and the U.S. blocking of aid to that country from international agencies. All these revelations led to the inevitable conclusion that the top echelons of the Nixon administration evinced a deep hostility toward the Allende government. Another conclusion was that the U.S. role in undermining and bringing down the Allende government was indeed major and direct, deplorable and counterproductive.

For many decades, Chile had a degree of cultural freedom rare in Latin America, and in the world as a whole. Freedom of speech and press were inviolable. Universities presented the widest scope of ideas. Academic freedom was widely respected. The publishing industry flourished. The clash of ideas, concepts, and theories was an integral part of the country's intellectual life. It was not considered the right or the function of the state to interfere with intellectual controversies or polemics.

As result of all these conditions, Chile had a highly sophisticated cultural life. The country's social scientists had high prestige; many of them gained international reputations. Chile's literary life was an exceedingly active one as well. Two Chileans won the Nobel Prize for Literature.

In the midst of this exemplary society, the U.S. sponsored a military coup against Allende and put an end to all this cultural excitement.

After all, who was Salvador Allende? Who was this man falsely portrayed by the American administration as a politically treacherous enemy of his own country and of the United States? How else could one expect Washington to describe him? In defiance of America's dollar diplomacy, Allende had the audacity to nationalize several major U.S. owned copper companies such as the Andes Copper, Chile Exploration Company, Anaconda, and Branden Copper.

Allende was born in Valparaiso, the son of an upper middle class family. After completing his medical studies, he helped found Chile's Socialist Party. He was later elected to congress where he developed a reputation as a 'champion of the poor.' In 1970, Allende ran for the presidency as the candidate of the Unidad Popular, a coalition of the socialists, communists, and other parties that included centrists and conservatives.

After winning, Allende called for desperately needed social and economic changes. Another policy that he sought actively was to continue traditional democratic political institutions.

His policies were aimed at improving conditions for the poor and restricting the role of corporations in the economy. In pursuing his goals, Allende increased the speed of land reforms, giving land to poor farmers. He nationalized many businesses including coal, steel and the vital copper industry. His policies caused prices to freeze and wages to rise. Allende subsidized milk and made certain that medical care and education were available for children.

PINOCHET GOVERNMENT

In the first days following the U.S. sponsored military coup; thousands of citizens were arrested. Many civilians were tortured in the National Stadium and in concentration camps throughout the country. The military ruled through a junta, headed by General Augusto Pinochet Ugarte. The junta suspended the constitution, dissolved congress, imposed censorship and banned all political parties. Concurrently, the junta began a campaign of terror against leftist elements.

More thousands were arrested; many tortured, executed or exiled. This despicable repression was intensified through the creation of a secret organization (DINA) specializing in making political activists disappear. Its high profile targets included General Carlos Prats, Allende's former Vice President, who was killed along with his wife by a bomb in Buenos Aires; Bernardo Leighton, founder of the Christian Democratic Party, machine gunned in Rome along with his wife; and Orlando Letelier, former Ambassador to the United States, who was murdered in Washington by a car bomb together with his assistant, Ronnie Moffit. Moffit had been lobbying to stop U.S. investment in Chile.

The key question here is how Pinchet's organization could manage to operate in our nation's capital and carry out an assassination without inside help.

For the next few years, the junta retained an iron grip on the country. Pinochet was head of the junta and the President, not merely Commander-in-Chief of the army but was himself, steeped in blood. Under Pinochet, Chile became the laboratory of economic neoliberalism. He managed to destroy the welfare state, as well as public health care and pensions. At the same time, the Pinochet family was considerably enriched.

CHAPTER XI

INDIAN WARS

The first declaration of the United States policy toward Native Americans was embodied in the Northwest Ordinance of 1787.

…"The utmost Good faith shall always be observed toward the Indians, their lands and property shall never be taken from them without their consent; and in their property, rights and liberty, they shall never be invaded or disturbed laws founded in justice and humanity shall from time to time be made, for preventing wrongs being done to them, and for preserving peace friendship with them."

How nefarious can history be?

The earliest contacts between the European settlers and the Native Americans were, for the most part, peaceful. Disputes were mostly resolved by negotiation or treaties, such as that made between Massasoit, Chief of the Wampanoag, and England's Plymouth Colony in 1621.

War with the Native Americans of New England was avoided until 1637. At this time, the Pequot War virtually exterminated that nation. The causes of this war, and of the English-Narragansett conflict of 1643-1645 and King Philip's War 1675-76, were the consequences of alleged violations of understandings, with both sides accusing the other.

In New England, Native Americans never regained the power that they possessed in the 17th century. They played important roles in King William's War (1689 to 1697,) Queen Anne's War (1702 to 1713,) and the French-Indian War (1754 to 1763.)

Each of the colonial powers in North America met Native America resistance. In the Southwest, the most notable incident was the ferocious Pueblo uprising precipitated by the Spanish and led by Popé in 1680. New France was constantly menaced by the hostility of the Iroquois Confederacy, although the French missionaries and traders maintained better relations with other northeastern tribes.

The history of the English settlements is studded with tribal conflicts. These conflicts included the war of the Pequot against Connecticut settlers in 1637; the uprising of the Wampanoag and Narragansett against the New England colonies; the wars with the Yamasee on the South Carolina frontier; as well as Pontiac's Rebellion in the Northwest territory in 1763.

In the South, when early European settlers arrived in what is now Jamestown, Virginia, local Native Americans, confederated under Chief Powhatan, were fully cooperative until the Europeans began to extend their settlements onto Native American land. Under Opechancanough, Powhatan's successor, Native Americans attacked the English settlements killing some three hundred and fifty colonists. The war ended in 1646 when the Governor, Sir William Berkeley, captured Opechancanough.

After the American Revolution, the most pressing Native American problem facing the new government was the unwillingness of the tribes of the Northwest to acquiesce in the settlement of the Ohio Valley. After unsuccessful expeditions under General Josiah Harmar and General Arthur St. Clair, the tribes of the Northwest Territory fought General Anthony Wayne and were defeated at the battle of Fallen Timbers in 1794.

One year later, by the Treaty of Greenville, the tribes agreed to give up their lands in Ohio. They also agreed to move to Indiana. Settlers soon began encroaching on Native American lands. It was here that Shawnee Chief Tecumseh, and his brother, the Shawnee Prophet, were provoked to organize a powerful native confederacy.

President William H. Harrison defeated the Shawnee Prophet at Tippecanoe in 1811. During the War of 1812, the Creek also rose. Andrew Jackson defeated them as well. After 1815, the policy of removing the indigenous population to a reservation across the Mississippi had great success. A great majority of the tribes had been relocated, but often only after a struggle. The attempts to remove the Seminole from their lands in Florida caused a number of wars; the most notable was the Seminole War involving the celebrated Osceola. Then the refusal of the Sac and Fox to be removed led to the Black Hawk War of 1832.

After 1860, wars continued but they now took place West of the Mississippi. In these conflicts, much of the fighting was done by the regular army, which was led by two renowned Indian fighters, General George Crook and General Nelson Miles. Most of the opposition came from four tribes: the Sioux, the Apache, the Comanche, and the Cheyenne. Other tribes that presented courageous, but futile, fighting against the white man's rapacity were the Arapaho, the Kiowa, the Ute, the Blackfoot, the Shoshone, the Nez Percé, and the Bannock. Among the Native American fighting leaders were Geronimo, Crazy Horse, Chief Joseph, Captain Jack, Red Cloud, and Mangas Coloradas.

The advance of the white settlers, with their wanton slaughter of the buffalo herds on which the Native Americans depended for their livelihood, caused numerous outbreaks of warfare in the West. The contributing factors were corrupt government agents, transgressions by prospectors seeking valuable minerals in tribal lands, and the interference of the railroads with the tribes' traditional hunting practices.

Hostilities between the army and indigenous tribes reached its height between 1869 and 1878. During this period, over two hundred pitched battles were fought. Although the Native Americans fought fiercely and with valor, the continuing flow of settlers to the West and the spread of a Western railroad network made their resistance ineffectual.

INDIAN REMOVAL (1814 to 1858)

Early in the 19th century, as the rapidly growing United States expanded into the lower South, white settlers faced what they considered an obstacle. This area was home to the Cherokee, Creek, Choctaw, Chickasaw and Seminole nations. In the view of the settlers, and many other white Americans, these Native Americans stood in the way of progress. Eager for land to raise cotton, the settlers pressured the federal government to acquire Indian Territory. Although relocating Native Americans had been going on since the early 1800s, it was given new impetus by the Indian Removal Act of 1830. This act was largely implemented during Andrew Jackson's presidency. This legislation resulted in the uprooting of entire tribes from their homelands and their forced resettlement to the west beyond the Mississippi.

Andrew Jackson, from Tennessee, was a forceful proponent of Indian removal. In 1814 he commanded the U.S. military forces that defeated a faction of the Creek nation. In their defeat, the Creeks lost twenty-two million acres of land in southern Georgia and central Alabama. The U.S. acquired even more land in 1818 when, spurred in part by the motivation to punish the Seminoles for their practice of harboring fugitive slaves, Jackson's troops invaded Spanish Florida.

From 1814 to 1824, Jackson was instrumental in negotiating nine treaties, which divested the southern tribes of their eastern lands in exchange for lands in the west. The tribes were coerced by the government to agree to the treaties on the grounds that in the west, they would be strategically better protected against white harassment. As result of these swindle treaties, the United States gained control over three-quarters of Alabama and Florida, as well as parts of Georgia, Tennessee, Mississippi, Kentucky and North Carolina.

The Supreme Court handed down a decision in 1823 under which Indians could occupy lands, however, they could not *hold title* to those lands. The reasoning behind this was that their 'right of occupancy' was subordinate to the United States' 'right of discovery.' In response to the great threat that this posed, the Creeks, Cherokee, and Chickasaw instituted policies of restricting land sales to the government. They wanted to protect what remained of their land before it was too late. Although the five Indian nations had made earlier attempts at resistance, most of their strategies were non-violent. One method was to adopt Anglo-American practices such as large scale farming, western education, and slave-holding. This method earned the nations the designation of 'the Five Civilized Tribes.' They adopted this policy of assimilation in an attempt to coexist with the settlers and to ward off hostility. Yet, it only made whites jealous and resentful.

Other attempts involved ceding portions of their land to the U.S. with a view of retaining control over at least part of their territory, or the territory they received in exchange. Some Indian nations simply refused to leave their land. The Creeks and the Seminoles even waged war to protect their territory. The First Seminole War lasted from 1817 to 1818. The Seminoles were aided by fugitive slaves who had found protection among them. The presence of the fugitives enraged the planters and fueled their desire to defeat the Seminoles.

The Cherokee used legal means in their efforts to safeguard their rights. They needed protection from land-hungry white settlers who continually harassed them by stealing their livestock. Further protection was needed when white settlers began burning their towns and squatting on their land.

In 1827, the Cherokee adopted a written constitution declaring themselves a sovereign nation. They did this because they knew that in former treaties Indian nations that had been declared sovereign were legally able to cede their lands. The Cherokee hoped to use the sovereign status to their advantage. However, the state of Georgia did not recognize it and continued to treat them as tenants living on state land. The Cherokee took the case to the Supreme Court, which ruled against them. In 1831, the Cherokee went to the Supreme Court again basing their appeal on an 1830 Georgia law which prohibited whites from living on Indian Territory. This time, the court ruled in favor of the Cherokee. However, Georgia refused to abide by the decision of the court. President Jackson refused to enforce the law.

Just a year after taking office, Jackson pushed 'The Indian Removal Act' through both houses of Congress. This act, which was created in 1830, resulted in the uprooting of entire tribes from their homelands and their forced resettlement beyond the Mississippi. Several wars stemmed from the refusal of some Native Americans to accept resettlement. The effort of the Sac (Sauk) and Fox to return to their homeland in early 1832 resulted in the Black Hawk

War in Illinois and Wisconsin. This war ended with the Bad Axe Massacre, in which most of the remaining Native Americans were killed as they tried to cross the Mississippi River into Iowa. Concurrently, the Cherokee were removed from Georgia, and in Mississippi and Alabama the remaining Creek were also expelled.

By the 1850s, only scattered groups of Native Americans remained in the eastern half of the United States. The Cherokee's removal from Georgia to Indian Territory became known as the Trail of Tears because nearly 4000 out of more than 18,000 who were forced from their homes, died in stockades or on their journey westward.

The U.S. government had relocated more than thirty eastern tribes to the West by the end of the 1830s. Although the government promised that Indian Territory would be a permanent home for these tribes, it violated its word, and again, the area became a part of the State of Oklahoma.

In December 1890, troops under the command of U.S. Army General Nelson A. Miles took a band of captive Sioux to a cavalry camp along Wounded Knee Creek. It was here that the federal troops killed three hundred seventy Sioux men, women, and children. This infamous act became known as the Wounded Knee Massacre.

The Gold Rush of 1849 brought devastation to the Native Americans of the Far West. The Bannock and Shoshone of Oregon and Idaho, the Ute of Nevada and Utah, and the Apache and Navajo of the Southwest mounted a resistance against white encroachment. They were, however, ultimately defeated and confined to reservations. The Arapaho, Cheyenne, and Sioux fought white encroachment on their territory in the 1860s and 1870s; the fighting was ferocious on both sides.

Among all the battles, only the Battle of the Little Bighorn is well known. On June 25, 1876, a combined force of Sioux and Cheyenne under Sioux Chief Sitting Bull and Chief Crazy Horse wiped out much of the 7th Cavalry Regiment under Lieutenant Colonel George Armstrong Custer. However, within a year most of the Sioux and Cheyenne surrendered. Some of them were relocated to Indian Territory. Other Native Americans such as Chief Joseph and the Nez Perce fought on into the late 1870s. Geronimo and the Apache continued fighting through the 1880s.

Most of the warfare ended with the massacre of the Indians at Wounded Knee, South Dakota on December 29, 1890, when the U.S. cavalry slaughtered Sioux warriors, women and children. The Native American resistance ended and the government confined them to reservations.

The writings of the French political writer and statesman, Alexis Charles Henri Maurice Clérel de Tocqueville (1805 to 1859,) on the political system of the United States became well-known worldwide. His work 'Democracy in America' is one of the most profound studies of American life and the influence of social and political institutions on the habits and manners of the people. He was highly critical of certain aspects of American democracy and believed for example, that public opinion tended toward tyranny and that majority rule could be as oppressive as the rule of a despot.

In his 'Present and future Condition of the Indians' he observed:…"Many attempts have been made to diffuse knowledge amongst the Indians, by the Jesuits of Canada and the Puritans in New England, leaving unchecked their wandering propensities. None of those endeavors were crowned by success. The Europeans continued to surround the Indians on every side, and to confine them within narrower limits and the Indians have been ruined by a competition which they had no means of sustaining. They were isolated in their own country, and their race constituted only a little colony in the midst of numerous and dominant people."

General Sherman summarized the cause of the Indian wars when he wrote: "We took away their country and their means of support broke up their mode of living, their habits of life, introduced disease and decay among them and it was for this and against this they made war. Could anyone expect less?"

EUGENE H. VAN DEE

CHAPTER XII

THE PHILIPPINES

More than four hundred years ago, on the Philippine island of Mactan, the European explorer Ferdinand Magellan was killed by a tribal chieftain, Lapu-Lapu. A few decades after Magellan's death, Spanish conquerors colonized the Philippine archipelago. Throughout the next three centuries, the Spanish rulers had to deal with uprisings of the native population. Filipino resistance to foreign domination was constant.

When in 1899, the U.S. military started to move beyond Manila in order to conquer and colonize the Philippines, the nationalists again resisted. A war ensued, proving that the essential ingredient of U.S. -Philippine relations in modern times was a war of conquest waged by America.

The resulting war, which lasted officially for three years and unofficially for at least twice as long, destroyed a fledgling Philippine republic. It turned the country into a U.S. colony bereft of the independence which it had won from Spain. The U.S. war had two main aims: to secure the Philippines as a market and source of raw materials for U.S. industry, and to secure the Philippines as a military strong-point from which to penetrate the markets of China. Another motive was one that was closely related to the feelings and theories of racial superiority which permeated the U.S. war effort.

Racial prejudice was evident in the cruel and brutal character of the U.S. war of conquest and marked by the use of torture, and the killing of prisoners. To isolate the guerilla fighters from their support in the countryside, the U.S. army thrust the rural population into concentration camps where great numbers died from hunger and disease. For the Philippine people, the war was a disaster. It snatched national independence from their grasp leaving hundreds of thousands of Filipinos dead. This war of colonial conquest was an exercise in imperial politics which established a pattern of U.S. intervention in other lands. All of this to further U.S. economic and military interests, while disregarding fundamental rules of warfare. The Americans were contemptuous of Filipinos. They had little respect for the fighting ability of their army. Jokingly, they called the battles 'quail shoots' referring to the Filipinos as 'niggers, barbarians, and savages.' This behavior reflected the racist and imperialist attitudes of American society at large.

Americans were elated by their success. General Elwell Otis confidently predicted that the war would end in a matter of weeks. This theme, trotted out by U.S. annexationists gave the impression that the war in the Philippines was but a slight variation of the Indian wars of the American West. However, there was another character to the fighting. It gradually dawned on the Americans in command that the more they had to disperse their forces, the more difficult it would become to defend themselves against counter-attack, ambush, and harassment by the highly mobile Philippine army.

The army itself was free of the need for the ponderous supply chain required by the Americans. The reason the Filipino troops could move around so easily without concern for a supply base and the reason information was so difficult to elicit from the native population were due to the fact that the Philippine nationalist cause had the total support of the Philippine masses.

The Americans began to realize that their major foe was not really the Philippine army. Instead, it was the Filipino people that were unrelentingly and implacably hostile to American imperialist designs. Guerilla activity was both on the rise and becoming increasingly effective. Being incessantly ambushed and harassed was nerve-wracking. The Americans began to exercise their mounting frustration on the population at large.

In April 1899, General Shafter gave grisly portent to the conduct of war: "it may be necessary to kill half of the Filipinos in order that the remaining half of the population may be advanced to a higher plane of life than their present barbarous state affords."

Reports of the burning of villages, the killing of non-combatants and the application of the 'water cure' to elicit information began to filter back to the U.S., often in letters from soldiers to their families which found their way to newspapers. A typical example: "On March 29th (1900) eighteen of my company killed seventy-five nigger bolo men and ten of the nigger gunners... When we find one who is not dead, we have bayonets..." Such atrocities were systematically denied by the War Department even when the evidence was irrefutable.

President McKinley also supported the annexation of Hawaii in 1898, after American businessmen had overthrown Hawaiian Queen Liliuokalani with the help of U.S. troops. Democratic President Grover Cleveland had found the action dishonorable and refused to annex the islands. McKinley saw the situation differently. "We need Hawaii just as much and a good deal more than we did California. It is manifest destiny," he said.

In 1899, by agreement with Britain and Germany, the United States also acquired the island of Tutuila in the Samoa islands. Its excellent harbor at Pago Pago became an important American naval station.

With the nomination of William Jennings Bryan as the Democratic presidential candidate, the question of American colonialism and military intervention appeared likely to become a major issue in the 1900 campaign. Hoping to topple the 'imperialistic party' of McKinley, the Filipinos launched an offensive that saw some of the fiercest fighting of the war. Still, the question of the Philippines never became the issue it should have been.

With the election safely out of the way, martial law was declared. American military operations were extended to Southern Luzon and to the Visayan islands where the Navy shelled coastal villages. The entire 51,000 population of Marinduque Island was ordered into five concentration camps set up by Americans.

An American congressman who had visited the Philippines spoke about the results of this campaign: "...you never hear of any disturbances in Luzon because there isn't anybody there to rebel... Our soldiers took no prisoners, they kept no records; they simply swept the country and wherever and whenever they could get hold of a Filipino they killed him."

By mid-summer 1901, the focus of the war started to shift south of Manila, where it was degenerating into mass slaughter. The Americans were simply chasing ragged, poorly armed guerillas, and inflicting the severest punishment on the people of the villages and barrios.

In the town of Balangiga, Samar, American troops had for some time been abusing the townspeople by packing them into open wooden pens at night where they were forced to sleep standing in the rain. One morning, guerilla bolo men infiltrated the town. The Balangiga killing of Americans initiated a reign of terror the likes of which had not yet been seen. General (Howlin Jake) Smith was chosen to lead the American mission of revenge. Smith's orders to his men were explicit: "Kill and burn, the more you kill and the more you burn, the more you please me."

While Smith ravaged Samar, Generals Malvar and Franklin Bell carried on massacres in Batangas, Laguna, Tayabas and Cavite. Bell issued a frightening series of orders and began setting up concentration camps, giving the people of Batangas only two weeks to move into them. The camps were overcrowded; the lack of food and clothing resulted in the spread of infectious diseases such as malaria, beriberi and dengue fever. Outside the camp, all property was destroyed; all houses put to the torch and the country became a 'desert waste.' By the time General Bell was finished more than 100,000 Filipinos-men, women and children had been killed or had died in Batangas. All of this was a direct result of the scorched-earth policies of the American military.

How many Filipinos died resisting American aggression? General Bell estimated in a *New York Times* interview that over 600,000 people in Luzon alone had been killed. Bell did not include those killed in the Panay campaign, the Samar campaign, or his own bloodthirsty Batangas campaign in which at least 100,000 died. Over a million deaths? Can one even imagine such carnage of innocent people who fought with extraordinary bravery in a just cause against an American aggressor?

On January 9, 1900, Senator Alfred J. Beveridge delivered a long speech to the U.S. Congress. 'Inter alia,' he said: "Mr. President, the times call for candor. The Philippines is ours forever... and just beyond the Philippines, are China's illimitable markets... We will not repudiate our duty to the archipelago. We will abandon our opportunity in the Orient. We will renounce our part in the mission of our race, trustee under God, of the civilization of the world... God has marked us as his chosen people, henceforth, to lead in the regeneration of the world. This island empire is the last land left in all the oceans. It should prove a mistake to abandon it. The blunder once made would be irretrievable."

Senator's Beveridge's speech was a definitive statement of the United State's war aims in the Philippines. It embraced all the main themes: the drive for markets, raw materials, and military strong points, the rivalry with other commercial powers, and the racist morality of white Anglo-Saxon supremacy. Some members, but there were only a few, accused Beveridge of being a bombastic windbag, an immoral proponent of the 'Manifest Destiny.' Nonetheless, his speech created a sensation in Washington.

Beveridge was not alone, however. In 1898, Senator Henry Cabot Lodge, a leader of the imperialist-minded group in the U.S. Senate, had already urged President McKinley, who had previously identified himself with U.S. business interests through his support of high tariffs, to hold the Philippines as a U.S. colony. "The domestic market is not enough," he told the President, "we must provide an additional market in the Philippines."

Lodge knew of course that McKinley's presidential campaign of 1896 had been the first in American history in which large corporations had intervened with massive financial support. In addition, much of the support for military action in the Spanish-American War had come from those who saw the newly freed countries as fresh markets for U.S. business. However, the people of the Philippines wanted American domination no more than they wanted Spanish domination. President McKinley had to suppress their insurrection against American occupation by using some 70,000 U.S. troops and more than $200 million to crush the resistance.

Washington granted the Philippines independence in 1946. Although colonialism was ending, Filipinos were not to be truly sovereign.U.S. economic domination would continue. The peasantry of the Central Luzon region and the veterans of the anti-Japanese struggle opposed this 'neocolonial' situation. They opposed even more strongly the exploitation they suffered at the hands of their landlords. Resentment and repression led to a new guerilla war, the Huk rebellion. The United States stepped in to help the Philippine elite defeat the Huks, thereby preserving U.S. interests and elite privilege.

CHAPTER XIII

CENTRAL INTELLIGENCE AGENCY

Senator J. William Fulbright, Chairman of the Senate Foreign Relations Committee, stated in 1971: "There exists in our nation today, a powerful and dangerous cult-the cult of intelligence. Its holy men are the clandestine professionals of the Central Intelligence Agency who have secrets and travel in a kind of fraternity, and they will not speak to anyone else. Its patrons and protectors are the highest officials of the federal government. Its membership, extending far beyond governmental circles, reaches into the power centers of industry, commerce, finance, and labor. Its friends are many in the areas of important public influence-the academic world and the media. The intelligence cult is a secret fraternity of American political aristocracy."

The purpose of the cult is to further the foreign policies of the United States government by covert and often illegal means. The cult's aim is to foster a world order in which America will rein supreme -the unchallenged international leader. Today, however, that dream is tarnished by both time and frequent failures, rendering the cult's objectives less grandiose, but no less disturbing.

The CIA is both the center and the primary instrument of the cult of intelligence. It engages in espionage, in disinformation, in psychological warfare and paramilitary activities. It penetrates and manipulates private institutions, and creates its own organizations, called 'proprietaries.' It recruits agents and mercenaries; it bribes and blackmails foreign officials to carry out its most unsavory tasks. It does whatever it deems required to achieve its goals, without any consideration of the ethics involved or the moral consequences of its actions. As the secret arm of American foreign policy, the CIA's most potent weapon is its covert intervention in the internal affairs of countries the U.S. government wishes to control or influence. The cult is intent on conducting the foreign affairs of the U.S. government without the awareness or participation of the people. Its adherents believe that only they have the right to decide what is necessary to satisfy the national needs and demands that it not be accountable for its actions to the people it professes to serve. The agency is privileged, as well as secret. In their minds, those who belong to the cult of intelligence have been ordained and their service immune from public scrutiny. The 'clandestine mentality' is a mind-set that thrives on secrecy and deception. It encourages professional amorality—the belief that goals can be achieved through the use of unprincipled means. Thus, the cult's leaders tenaciously guard their actions from public view. With the cooperation of an acquiescent Congress, and the assistance of a series of presidents, the cult has built a wall of laws and executive orders around the CIA. This wall blocks any effective public scrutiny. Members of the cult of intelligence have frequently lied to protect the CIA and to hide their own responsibility for its operations.

The Eisenhower administration also lied to the American people about the CIA's involvement in the Guatemalan *coup d'état* in 1954, about the agency's support of the unsuccessful rebellion in Indonesia in 1958, and the Francis Powers 1960 U-2 mission. The Kennedy administration lied about the CIA's role in the abortive invasion of Cuba in 1961, admitting its involvement only after the operation had failed disastrously. The Johnson administration lied about the extent of U.S. government and CIA commitments in Vietnam and Laos. The Nixon administration publicly lied about the agency's attempt to fix the 1970 Chilean election and its role in the assassination of its President. George W. Bush lied to the American Congress, to the United Nations, to the Prime Minister of Britain Tony Blair, and to the American people about Iraq's weapons of mass destruction and the imperative need to invade that country. (Again we hear the echo of nearly identical rhetoric espoused by President James Polk about Mexico over 150 years ago.)

For the adherents to the cult of intelligence, hypocrisy and deception have become standard techniques for preventing public awareness of the CIA's clandestine operations and governmental accountability. The agency's members ask that they be regarded as honorable citizens and true patriots. Then, when caught in webs of their own deceit these same people assert that the government has an inherent right to lie to its people.

The original mission of the CIA was to coordinate the intelligence of various governmental departments and agencies, and to produce reports helpful to the national leadership in conducting the affairs of U.S. foreign policy. That was Truman's view. However, General William 'Wild Bill' Donovan, Allen Dulles and other veterans of the wartime Office of Strategic Services (OSS) thought differently. They saw the Agency as the clandestine instrument by which Washington could achieve foreign policy goals not attainable through diplomacy.

The American public does not realize how frequently the CIA failed. The CIA's Clandestine Services have been singularly unsuccessful in penetrating or spying on many major targets. The only espionage operation against the Soviets that the Agency can point to with any pride was the

Penkovsky case in the early 1960s. However, the information that made it possible was literally handed over to the CIA by British Intelligence.

KGB defector Oleg Penkovsky was the most valuable resource ever to come to the CIA from inside Russia. Penkovsky provided the first reliable intelligence about Soviet nuclear capabilities, and in so doing, provided the White House with the backbone to stand up to the Soviets in the confrontations over Berlin and Cuba. So how did the CIA manage to lose Penkovsky?

The CIA's ability to deal properly with Soviet defectors had already been poisoned by the Byzantine conspiracy theories of the Agency's half-mad, Counter-Intelligence Chief, James J. Angleton. An earlier KGB defector, Anatoly Golitsin, convinced Angleton that any Soviet who followed him would be a plant and that there was a Soviet mole in the CIA's chain of command.

Angleton tore the Agency apart looking for the mole, ruining the careers of scores of CIA officers and vigorously attempting to discredit Penkovsky. He then imprisoned an important defector, Yuri Nosenko, and in time paralyzed the agency's Soviet division. Again, the dimwitted CIA botched it.

At about the time that Kennedy confronted the Soviets about Cuba, the KGB arrested Penkovsky. Penkovsky had been under surveillance for months, burned by the CIA's inability to provide experienced contacts or safe sites in Moscow where he could deposit information. He begged the CIA to exfiltrate him. The Agency would not. Penkovsky was tried and shot. His capture was facilitated by the fact that the CIA Station Chief in Moscow, Paul Garbler, knew almost nothing about the Penkovsky operation.

Garbler was not told that a 'dead drop' (a secret location for passing materials to and from Penkovsky) was under KGB surveillance, though CIA headquarters knew it. Why was Garbler cut out of the loop? He had fallen victim to Angleton's paranoia and tagged as a 'potential Soviet agent.'

Had the CIA not gone down, over the years, a thousand blind alleys, it could have developed a clearer understanding of the Soviets long before Soviet policy defeated itself. Additionally, had presidents and policy makers achieved that understanding, then America's costly standoff with the Soviet Union might have been avoided and our economic fortunes might have vastly improved.

The very fact that the United States operates an active CIA around the world has done incalculable harm to the nation's international position. Not only have millions of people abroad been alienated by the CIA activities, but so have a large number of Americans, especially young people.

Malcolm Muggeridge, renowned for his observations on the foibles and follies of modern man's futile search for contentment wrote: "In the eyes of posterity, it will inevitably seem that in safeguarding our freedom, we destroyed it; that the vast clandestine apparatus we built to probe our enemies' resources and intentions only served in the end to confuse our own purposes and that the practice of deceiving others for the good of the state led infallibly to our deceiving ourselves; and that the huge army of intelligence personnel created to execute these purposes were soon caught up in the web of their own sick fantasies."

Newsweek Magazine once described the CIA as the most ineffective organization in American society, practicing secrecy to prevent the American public from learning of its activities. It further stated that the agency's true purpose has been warped by the need to nourish a collective clandestine ego.

A few years ago, senior officials of the CIA gathered in a conference room at its headquarters in Langley, Virginia. The purpose of the meeting was to address the worst situation that an intelligence service can ever face, the blown cover of its operatives. One by one CIA agents in the Soviet bloc code named Tickle, Blizzard, Gentile and Pyrric had been uncovered and apprehended by the Communists. Those arrested included the London Station Chief of the KGB, a Red Army General, and most of the rest of the CIA's top Soviet agents active in the 1980s.

CIA operations in Russia were in ruins. One of the officials jokingly remarked: "someone in this room must be a mole." Everyone laughed; including the CIA veteran responsible for blowing the agents covers, a man named Aldrich Hazen Ames.

The arrest of Ames, Chief of CIA's Soviet counter-intelligence branch provoked outrage from security hawks and derision from CIA critics. Both groups had the same question: How the hell could the Agency have missed Ames' activities when he was driving a Jaguar, buying a fancy house with $540,000 in cash, lying to his superiors about his overseas travels, and having trouble passing lie detector tests?

Part of the answer, one that nobody paid attention to, was that the CIA is far too much of a private club. It is an organization whose members take care of each other and pledge allegiance to their own community. This *clubbiness* protected Ames who, as the son of a CIA officer, was legendary. This clique mentality also prevented the Agency and its outside overseers from dealing with CIA shortcomings, both large and small.

William Colby, CIA Director from 1973 to 1976, observed that such clandestine bonding caused many people to drop out of ordinary society and to immerse themselves exclusively in a cloak-and dagger lifestyle. Out of that, grew an inbred, distorted, elitist view of intelligence that held itself above the normal processes and rules of society. The agency had its own rationale and justification beyond the restraints of the Constitution which applied to everyone else.

Stanfield Turner, President Carter's much maligned CIA Director, mused on the impact of covert life: "Hiding your accomplishments, leading a double life, regularly confronted with moral issues can all take their toll. In many ways, a clandestine career deforms the person involved and the institution itself."

Five weeks after he took over the CIA, Turner was flabbergasted when he read in *The Washington Post* that Edwin Wilson, another CIA official, had become a rogue arms dealer with ties to Libyan strongman Muammar Qaddafi. This all took place while Wilson still had active relationships with other Agency officials.

Turner was even more shocked to learn that months before, during the tenure of CIA Chief George Bush, the Inspector General's office had learned of Wilson's relationship with the CIA men and did nothing. No one even seemed concerned. Turner summoned to his office the top officials of the Agency: Deputy Director E. Henry Knoche, Deputy for Operations William Wells, Inspector General John Waller, Theodore Shackley, and others.

"Gentlemen," Turner said, "the question is what to do about the two CIA employees who had worked with Wilson." The choices were exoneration, punishment, or dismissal.

All of the career officials recommended a modest punishment, arguing that dismissal would demoralize the

Agency. Only Robert "Rusty" Williams, a CIA outsider, brought in by Turner to be his assistant, favored canning the pair. It was an eye opening moment for Turner. *'These fellows,'* he thought, 'are too damned protective of each other. '

The covert world's clannishness allows its members not only a little slack, but it also keeps some of the club's biggest secrets totally hidden. Testifying in a federal district court, Ames stated that the "espionage business, as conducted out by the CIA, was a self-serving sham, carried out by careerist bureaucrats who have managed to deceive several generations of American policy makers about the value of their work. Thousands of case officers and tens of thousands of agents around the world," Ames maintained, "have been spinning their wheels, providing information irrelevant to policy makers' needs; our espionage establishment having transformed itself into a self serving interest group immeasurably aided by secrecy."

In key theaters, the CIA compiled a miserable performance record. It flopped completely in attempting to recruit significant spies in the Soviet bloc. It failed to infiltrate Fidel Castro's ruling group and did not discover that the Soviets were installing missiles in Cuba (this information actually came from a Cuban refugee in Florida.) Intelligence in Vietnam was a farce because the CIA never penetrated the higher reaches of the enemy, nor did it fully comprehend the weaknesses of the Saigon regime.

The Soviets used the CIA's meddling in the affairs of other countries to great effect. The USA was seen as imperialistic and hypocritical. What more evidence was needed than the fact that it would overthrow a legally elected leader such as Jacobo Arbenz of Guatemala after he nationalized 400,000 acres of idle banana plantation land owned by the U.S. United Fruit Company?

Of course this lead to an investigation by the Senate, that is supposed to have intelligence oversight. The Senate Select Committee was to Study Governmental Operations with respect to intelligence activities. This group, known as the Church Committee, revealed that the United States had participated in plots to assassinate foreign leaders, including Castro. The Church Committee did not definitely state that Presidents Eisenhower or Kennedy authorized the plots, but a number of Senators, including Howard Baker, felt certain that the CIA operated with presidential approval.

The Castro assassination plots continued after the Cuban missile crisis. On November 22, 1963, CIA agents met in Paris with a traitorous Cuban official, Rolando Cubela Secades. The agents gave him a ballpoint pen rigged with a poisonous hypodermic needle intended to cause Castro's instant death. Desmond Fitzgerald of CIA's Directorate of Plans assured Cubela that the CIA operated with the full approval of Attorney General Robert F. Kennedy. The Church Committee further disclosed that on June 19, 1963, President Kennedy approved a sabotage program against Cuba. This program included thirteen major operations among them attacks on an electric power plant, an oil refinery, and a sugar mill.

Historian Arthur Meier Schlesinger wrote in his biography of Robert Kennedy, that Kennedy knew of CIA support for militaristic Cuban exiles, such as Manuel Artime, ("when it came to Cuba, the attorney general was ever the activist, constantly exclaiming that the administration must do something about Castro.")

Schlesinger also acknowledged that the Attorney General received in May 1962 an extensive oral briefing about CIA efforts to encourage U.S. gambling syndicate members Salvatore Giancana and John Rosselli to organize Castro's assassination.

CHAPTER XIV

JAPANESE INTERNMENT

The internment of Japanese Americans by the U.S. government is one of the most extraordinary blows to constitutional rights in the history of our nation. From 1942, to 1946, some 120,000 persons of Japanese ancestry, of whom 77,000 were American citizens, were denied their rights to life, liberty, and property without any criminal charges being filed against them.

The entire West Coast Japanese American population was forced from its homes. They were confined to internment camps in deserts and swamplands. Japanese American men, women and children, including the elderly and the disabled, had to sell or abandon their possessions and leave their friends to live humiliated behind barbed wire.

The basis for the government's policy was the unconscionable presumption that this group of people, solely because of their ancestry, had to be inherently disloyal to the United States. This presumption reflected a long-standing history of American anti-Asian prejudice. It was the climax of a long history of racism on the West Coast directed against Asian immigrants.

Those from China, felt the first blows of this white supremacist attitude in the second half of the 1880s. Evidence of official bias included the Federal Chinese Exclusion Act of 1882, as well as the massacre of twenty-eight Chinese miners in Wyoming at the hands of white miners fearful of labor competition.

The very first drug law in the history of the United States had little to do with illegal drugs. The purpose of the California legislation was clearly aimed at keeping the Chinese from gathering, as they did in opium dens in San Francisco.

As Japanese immigration increased after the virtual cutoff of Chinese immigrants, discriminatory efforts targeted this new "yellow peril."

The majority of the first Issei, or first-generation Japanese in America, worked in the California farming industry. Although they began as farm laborers, they gradually saved enough money to buy their own land. As the worked and then owned more land, the laborers became an integral part of the California agricultural industry. Their accomplishments were truly amazing.

While they made up only two percent of the population, they controlled roughly 450,000 acres of farmland, producing ninety percent of some valuable crops. With their skills and knowledge, Issei farmers were able to open up new lands with their labor intensive high-yield style of agriculture, far more effective than the resource-intensive characteristics of American farming. Thus, the Japanese farmers helped to revolutionize agriculture. They also greatly contributed to California's ascension as an agricultural Mecca.

Nevertheless, the white community viewed the success of the Japanese in agriculture as fierce and unwanted competition. The anti-Asian sentiments that once terrorized Chinese immigrants now focused on the Japanese. First manifested as verbal abuse and violence, the prejudices against them became institutionalized in law by local, state, and federal governments.

The California State Legislature passed the Alien Land Law in 1913 prohibiting aliens from buying land or leasing it for more than three years. The bill was designed to keep the Japanese out of the landowning class, declaring unlawful ownership of real property by "aliens ineligible for citizenship."

Other laws were passed that denied citizenship to the Japanese. They were officially barred from marrying Caucasians. But prejudice against Japanese Americans rose to even greater heights after World War II began.

Special Investigative Reports presented to congress by the FBI, the U.S. military and naval intelligence clearly stated that almost one hundred percent of the Japanese people were trustworthy. These reports were not revealed to the American public until after the war ended, and only after 120,000 people of Japanese descent had been incarcerated in American concentration camps.

Because of the long pernicious history of prejudice against Japanese Americans, the general population began to believe fabricated stories about Japanese spies. The William Randolph Hearst's newspapers vigorously attacked Japanese Americans. Henry McLemore, a syndicated Hearst columnist, wrote on January 29, 1942, "I hate the Japanese and am for the immediate removal of every Japanese on the West Coast..."

Other articles with similar messages and fabricated stories about Japanese agents were published. Groups such as the American Legion, the Native Sons of the Golden West and the California State Grange, vocally expressed their desire for the evacuation and incarceration of all Japanese Americans. The California delegation to the Congress urged President Roosevelt to remove the entire West Coast Japanese population. That idea was also supported by Lt. General John Lesesne DeWitt, and California Attorney

General Earl Warren, who later became the Governor of California.

Actually, throughout the course of the entire war, not one episode of espionage or sabotage was committed by a Japanese American. That didn't seem to matter. With the backing of Congress and the President, DeWitt began to implement, in March 1942, his plan to "rid the West Coast of all persons of Japanese ancestry."

The plan called for all people of Japanese ancestry in California, parts of Arizona, Washington, and Oregon to turn themselves in at temporary detention centers. These were mainly converted fairgrounds, race tracks, and livestock exhibition halls. In some cases, horse stalls, which had housed animals only weeks before, were used as living quarters for the evacuated Japanese Americans. The evacuees typically received notice of evacuation only a few days prior to the required departure date. They were allowed to take only those belongings that they could carry. Property and other possessions had to be hurriedly sold for much less than their value, abandoned or given away.

For the Japanese Americans, this was the destruction of a dream -the American dream -as they lost what they had worked so hard for years to gain. If the purpose of the evacuation orders was to protect the West Coast against espionage and sabotage, how can we account for the infants, elderly and physically ill people who were included in the detentions?

By June of 1942, following the Battle of Midway in the Pacific, the U.S. government and its military leaders were aware that any danger of a Japanese invasion was effectively over. But the building of relocation camps continued in Manzanar and Tule Lake in California, Poston and Gila River in Arizona, Rohwer and Jerome in Arkansas, Minidoka in

Idaho, Heart Mountain in Wyoming, Topaz in Utah, and Granada (Amache) in Colorado.

Each of the camps held between 8,000 and 16,000 evacuees. An approximate total of 120,000 people were ultimately detained. Prisoners were enclosed by high barbed-wire fences and armed soldiers kept watch. Large families were squeezed into tiny un-partitioned rooms, the largest being twenty by twenty-four feet with no running water or plumbing, forcing internees to use simple latrines.

While Japanese Americans were detained in the camps, Congress proposed blatantly racist legislation. One bill proposed to divest all American born Japanese Americans of their citizenship. It was designed in order to send them to Japan at the war's end. One representative even suggested a mandatory sterilization program. All this must have made General DeWitt feel like the spiritual brother of Heinrich Himmler. Himmler as head of the infamous German police and the most ruthless of Nazi leaders supported the very same concept for Jews in Europe. Himmler was chiefly responsible for Nazi extermination camps during World War II.

Actually, in the annals of that war and in history books, DeWitt is described as the military leader responsible for the worst abuses of civil liberties in the history of the United States.

Forty-five hundred Japanese men from Hawaii and the mainland voluntarily joined U.S. forces. They formed a segregated unit. This unit, combined with the 100th Battalion, became the 442nd Regimental Combat Team. In seven major campaigns, over 18,000 men served with the 442nd which had a three hundred percent casualty rate and became the most decorated unit of its size in World War II.

It received seven Presidential Distinguished Unit Citations and earned 18,143 individual decorations, including one Congressional Medal of Honor, 47 Distinguished Service Crosses, 350 Silver Stars, 810 Bronze Stars, and more than 3,600 Purple Hearts. Although the 442nd is the best known Japanese American contribution to the war, altogether over 33,000 Nisei served in the nation's military forces. Ironically, they were fighting for the country that held their families in concentration camps.

CHAPTER XV

HIROSHIMA AND NAGASAKI

As the war with Germany drew closer to the end, the Allies waged an increasingly effective war against Japan. After the fall of the Mariana Islands including Saipan to the U.S. in July 1944, and the American naval blockade which was strangling Japan's ability to import oil and other raw material to produce weapons, the imminent defeat of Japan became apparent to both American and Japanese Leaders. Admiral William Leahy, the Chief of Staff to Roosevelt and then to Truman, wrote, "By the beginning of September 1944, Japan was almost completely defeated through a total sea and air block."

The surrender of Germany in May 1945 freed the Allies to focus their troops and resources on vanquishing the final enemy, Japan. In August of that year, the Soviet Union invaded Manchuria after having advised Japan's ambassador to Moscow that as of August 9th, the Soviet Union would be at war with Japan.

Both, General Eisenhower and Admiral Leahy, opposed using the Atomic Bomb, believing it was no longer necessary. Nonetheless, President Truman authorized its use. On August 6, 1945, a B-29 named *Enola Gay,* under the command of Colonel Paul W. Tibbets, began to roll down a runway on Tinian Island on its historic mission to destroy Hiroshima. The plane carried a crew of twelve men and an atomic bomb fueled with Uranium 235. As it flew over Iwo Jima, the mission was joined by two other B-29s; their crews would seek scientific information on the blast and take photographs.

The *Enola Gay* encountered no resistance from anti-aircraft or enemy fighters. The fleet of just three caused little alarm, no warning signals sounded and the Japanese saw no reason to seek shelter.

The Enola Gay's bombardier released the bomb, equivalent in power to 14,000 tons of TNT. Even at 30,000 feet (eleven miles) from ground zero, the plane was hit by two strong shock waves. The waves bounced the plane around like a piece of metal.

On the ground, the bomb produced a ghastly scene of desolation, ruin and human suffering. 4.4 square miles surrounding ground zero were completely devastated. The tremendous flash scorched concrete, leaving the silhouettes of vaporized human beings. It melted away the eyeballs of people looking in the direction of the blast. The number of people in the city, including transients, conscripted workers and Japanese troops, was about 350,000. The number of deaths was estimated at 130,000 including later victims of radiation. Many survivors were horribly debilitated. Blinded by the flash, burned and blistered by the heat, cut beyond recognition by flying glass, those who could move, stumbled through the darkness caused by dust, smoke, and debris.

Charred bodies were everywhere. No services were available to help the living out of the fires, to salve their wounds, or even to ease their agony. Those survivors who received large doses of radiation died within a short time; others who received less exposure, developed cancer or other causes of premature death.

Three days after Hiroshima, another B-29 named *Bock's Car* dropped a plutonium bomb on Nagasaki; in that second blast some 70,000 people lost their lives. Significantly, it was not until the day after the second bomb was used that leaflets, prepared after Hiroshima, were dropped on Nagasaki. These announcements warned Japanese citizens about atomic attacks. Was this America's revenge for Pearl Harbor?

In Potsdam, Germany, where he was attending a summit conference with Churchill and Stalin, President Truman, according to Secretary of war Stimson, was "tremendously pepped up" by the news of the successful mission.

Was the atomic bomb necessary to compel Japan to surrender? Or were the merciless bombardment of the Japanese coast and the strangling blockade of Japan by the Pacific fleet the key factors? Was the ferocious fire bomb raids on Japan's cities by fleets of B-29s the enough to make Japan surrender? The use of nuclear weapons to destroy Hiroshima and Nagasaki was the culmination of a policy of firebombing and napalming Japanese cities after strategic bombing failed to incapacitate Japanese industry.

Even before the atomic bombs fell, every major city in Japan was already badly damaged. More than 500,000 civilians were killed in these earlier attacks. A single raid on Tokyo in March 1945 destroyed vast areas of the city, killed 100,000 people, injured many more, and created nearly one million refugees. Thousands died from smoke inhalation, anoxia, or carbon monoxide poisoning, or were boiled to death when the firestorm heated the waters. General Thomas Power termed it the greatest single disaster incurred by any enemy in military history.

Despite the destruction of defenseless cities, the elimination of all important industrial concentrations, the virtual paralysis of Japanese air and naval forces, the American attacks continued. No significant discussion of the ethics of civilian bombing took place either in policy councils or in the public domain. The atomic bombing of Hiroshima and Nagasaki was devoid of any ethical consideration.

CHAPTER XVI

DRESDEN

City and Capital of Saxony, Dresden is the third largest city in eastern Germany. On the division of Saxony in 1485, it became the residence and capital of the Albertine line of Wettin rulers. After a disastrous fire in 1491, the electors rebuilt and modernized the city in the Baroque and Rococo styles. During the reign of August the Strong, Dresden emerged as one of Europe's leading cultural centers.

Because of its stimulating intellectual and cultural atmosphere, Dresden became a center of the Romantic movement and of the Romantic school of painting. The Baroque beauty of the city, along with its splendid art collections, attracted many great scholars, philosophers, composers. Many of the artists of the period made Dresden their home.

The Saxon State Orchestra, founded in 1548, possessed an extraordinary history and tradition and was considered among the greatest orchestras of Europe. The great composer, Richard Wagner, served as music director, conducting the first performances of his own *creations: Rienzi, The Flying Dutchman* and *Tannhauser.*

Heavily damaged during the Seven Years War (1756 to 1763), the city was partially rebuilt. Thereafter, it was known as the Florence of the Elbe River. Because of its magnificent architecture and outstanding museums, Dresden was numbered among the world's most beautiful cities.

When war broke out in Europe in September 1939, President Roosevelt immediately appealed to the governments of Great Britain, France, and Germany to refrain from "ruthless bombing of civilians in unfortified centers of population." As praiseworthy as this plea seemed to be at the time, it became an albatross later when the United States engaged in massive bombing raids.

The U.S.-British bombing of Dresden, an undefended city with no significant war industry, remains the single best known and most widely condemned example of firebombing and the deliberate annihilation of civilian populations in the history of warfare.

On February 13, 1945, 1,400 British aircraft followed by 1,350 U.S. bombers destroyed Dresden and unleashed a firestorm visible two hundred miles away. The destruction of Dresden, killing 135,000 German civilians, was the prelude to another wave of U.S. B-29 firebomb and napalm attacks that sowed destruction and extracted a heavy toll in human life in Germany in the spring and summer of 1945. This revealed again that the nation who wishes to call another nation to task for violating the laws of humanity should, like Caesar's wife, be above reproach.

CHAPTER XVII

INTERVENTION IN SOMALIA

With a population of eight million, Somalia is directly south of the Arabian Peninsula across the Gulf of Aden, in extreme East Africa. Mogadishu is the capital of Somalia. Between the 7th and 10th century immigrant Muslim Arabs and Persians established trading posts along Somalia's Gulf of Aden and Indian Ocean coasts.

Between the 15th and 16th centuries, Somali warriors regularly joined the armies of the Muslim sultanates in their battles with Christian Ethiopia. British, French, and Italian imperialism all played an active role in the region in the 19th century.

France first acquired a foothold in the area in the 1860s. Italy first asserted its authority there in 1889 by creating a small protectorate in the central zone to which other areas ceded by the sultan of Zanzibar were later added in the south.

In 1960, by agreement with the U.N. Trusteeship Council, Somalia was granted independence. Ten years later, General Mohamed Siad Barre seized power and declared Somalia a socialist state. After being deposed and fleeing Somalia, Barre died in 1995 in Lagos, Nigeria.

On December 4, 1992, President George Bush agreed to send some 30,000 U.S. military forces to Somalia under the auspices of the United Nations "Operation Restore Hope." U.S. Marines went ashore in Mogadishu a week later. For the first time American military were formally deployed by the commander-in-chief, allegedly for humanitarian reasons, rather than for securing vital strategic, political or economic interests.

Despite U.S. government disclaimers, some commentators were convinced that "Operation Restore Hope" marked the beginning of a new interventionist doctrine in which the United States, acting under the cover of the United Nations, attempted to fulfill its self proclaimed mission of "bringing orderliness" to the post-Cold-War world.

Assuming that Washington only commits U.S. military forces to situations where vital American interests are at risk, why the rush to intervene in Somalia? Is it that the United Nations has become a rubber-stamp institution, simply providing the legitimized facade behind which Washington can seek to maintain the international status quo or punish those who threaten to challenge the post-Cold-War order? Actually, with no countervailing power to contain the United States in the new world order, Washington was embarking upon a new global crusade against radicalism in the Third World.

The circumstances leading to U.S. military intervention in Somalia are both tragic and ironic. Nature and man have conspired to create a tragedy whose ramifications will be felt for generations. As result of drought and internal conflict, one third of Somalia's seven million people were in danger of perishing from starvation and disease.

During 1992, an estimated 300,000 Somalis had died of malnourishment or violence. The irony of the Somali tragedy is that on the surface, Somalia appeared to be one of the least vulnerable states to the type of ethnic conflict that destabilized other African countries, owing to the homogeneity of the Somali people.

While Somalia was seen as possessing a cohesive national foundation upon which to build a relatively stable political system, its irredentist claims became a source of great anxiety and international instability in the Horn of Africa. The principle of inviolability of colonial borders embodied in the 1963 Organization of African Unity (OAU) was principally aimed at Somalia.

In effect, the OAU Charter made the Somalis the outlaws of Africa. Somalia seemed to live up to its reputation, provoking border clashes with Kenya and Ethiopia, making threatening moves toward Djibouti in 1977, just as it was about to gain independence from France. The Somalis also launched a full scale invasion of Ogaden in 1977 and infiltrated the area again with regular army forces in 1980. Not surprisingly, a unified and well-armed Somalia was viewed by its neighbors as the most dangerous entity in the Horn.

There is no question that the United States is one of the 'criminals' who flooded Somalia with arms. Beginning with 1980 through 1989, the U.S. provided Somalia with more than $125 million in the Military Assistance Program, $200 million in Economic Support Funds, $60 million in financing credits, $200 million in cash guarantees, and some $7 million in International Military Education and Training. This program would train more than three hundred and fifty Somali military students.

What did Washington hope to gain by intervening in Somalia? It would be difficult to find anyone among U.S. policy makers who would argue that the Horn of Africa, let alone Somalia, is of vital strategic importance to the United States. The Henry Kissinger school of thought that strategic interest, not humanitarian need, is the driving reason for deploying forces overseas is still the predominant mindset among U.S. national security planners.

In his forward to *Mogadishu! Heroism and Tragedy,* Ross Perrot wrote: "Read this book carefully. Never forget its contents as you watch the TV docu-dramas of smart bombs going down air shafts, where war is presented in a sterile, sanitized environment. Remember, war is fighting and dying." Notable by its absence from this sentence is the verb "killing." Operation Restore Hope was launched amid shocking -and carefully orchestrated U.S. images of anarchy and starvation in Somalia, with the mandate of "creating a secure environment for the delivery of humanitarian relief."

Instead, eight months later it turned into the greatest humiliation of the U.S. military since Vietnam. In three months of urban counter-guerilla warfare against the unpaid, irregular but resourceful militia of General Mohammed Farah Aidid in Mogadishu City, U.S. military doctrines of overwhelming force and near-zero American casualties came apart.

The culmination was the battle during which a dead U.S. pilot was dragged through the streets by a jeering crowd. It forced a truce and U.S. withdrawal. This operation, in which all humanitarian principles were wholly ignored, had more to do with upholding the prestige of the United Nations in the world where its credibility was severely compromised than with seeking solutions to Somalia's problems.

The collapse of the U.S. intervention can only be understood when it is realized just how deeply the U.S. forces had antagonized a wide swathe of Somali society. When the marines first landed on the Mogadishu beaches, hopes were high that they would solve the country's problems. However, not only had they disappointed the Somalis on that promise, but the behavior of a large number of the troops was deplorable. In many cases, the operations quickly degenerated into routine brutality against Somali civilians. Abuses by U.S. forces were not only caused by the frustration of front-line troops. They were also the direct and inevitable outcome of decisions made high up in military command. For this reason, the U.S. has been conspicuously unwilling to open any sort of inquiry into the conduct of its forces.

The importance of this inglorious circumstance in American military history lies not only in the carnage among the residents of Somalia's capital city but what it tells us about U.S. military doctrine. It also sheds light on some of the reasons behind U.S. administration's efforts to block the creation of an independent International Crime Court with universal jurisdiction to investigate war crimes and crimes against humanity.

EUGENE H. VAN DEE

CHAPTER XVIII

KOREA

The Korean War originated with the division of Korea into South and North Korea after World War II (1939-1945.) In 1948, the South proclaimed the Republic of Korea and the North established the People's Republic of Korea. North Korean forces crossed the dividing line in 1950 and invaded the South. In defense of the South, the United States joined the fighting under the banner of the United Nations, along with contingents of British, Canadian, Australian and Turkish troops.

In October 1950, China joined the war on the North's side. By the time a cease fire agreement was signed on July 27, 1953, millions of soldiers and civilians had perished. The armistice ended the fighting. Nevertheless, Korea has remained divided for the decades since and is subject to the possibility of a new war at any time.

The Korean conflict placed great stress on the Western alliance that had developed after World War II. European leaders were worried that the conflict might place pressure on them from Washington to rearm, something they could not afford. They also feared that Europe could become the battleground for a war between the United States and the Soviet Union. Many of them also resented the unilateral manner in which the United States conducted the Korean War and the power General MacArthur appeared to assert over the Pentagon and the White House. They also worried about the influence right-wing elements had in the United

States. In no nation were these concerns more evident than in Great Britain.

There can be no doubt that over the past half century, London has been the United State's closest ally. However, during the Korean War, London and Washington's opinions differed on a number of issues, especially with regard to the Chinese after they entered the war. While London always supported Washington publicly, privately Britain sought to convince the United States to moderate some of its more militarily dangerous inclinations, which may have also helped speed up the peace process.

Yet, the result of the war was to tarnish Anglo-American relations as well as the U.S. relations with other Western European allies. However, after North Korea invaded South Korea, and the United States made clear its intentions not to let the invasion go unchallenged, there was never any doubt that Western Europe would support Washington's position at the United Nations.

Britain voted in support of a Security Council Resolution sponsored by the United States calling for an international military action to defend South Korea. Not only was London anxious to cement its 'special relationship' with Washington, it was concerned that if the attack in Korea went unanswered, the Soviet Union might feel free to move into Iran, where vital British oil interests would be threatened.

Promptly, Britain placed its air and naval units stationed in Japan under the command of General Douglas MacArthur, commander of U.N. forces in Korea. France undertook to raise fifteen divisions and the Netherlands also committed forces, as did Australia, New Zealand, and Canada.

U.S. intelligence agencies concluded that China would not enter the war. The CIA decided that "the odds are that

Communist China, like the USSR, will not openly intervene in North Korea."

MacArthur swept confidently onward and captured the North Korean capital. What he did not know was that three days earlier, the Chinese had crossed the Yalu River into North Korea. After this was confirmed, alarm bells went off throughout Europe. The British were determined that the United States must avoid war with China. They urged the establishment of a buffer zone between China and Korea.

U.S. Secretary of State Dean Acheson, spoke out against the plan. He maintained that the zone could be used by the Chinese as a staging area for the further buildup of their forces. Acheson even raised the possibility that the United States might have to send aircraft across the border in order to defend the airspace over the Yalu River.

The British warned that they would withdraw their forces from the United Nations Command if Washington forced Beijing into an all out war.

The massive Chinese offensive and the retreat of the Eighth Army from the Yalu River had a profound effect on Europeans. The confidence in General MacArthur was badly shaken. After inspecting the battlefields, British General Leslie Mansergh delivered a secret report to the British Chiefs of Staff. In his speech, he criticized American forces for their "lack of determination (and) their inability to stand and fight."

MacArthur became a symbol for most European leaders of what was wrong with America's foreign policy. He was bitterly attacked for wanting to escalate the fighting in Asia while Europe was left virtually defenseless. Europeans were terribly afraid that the Korean conflict might escalate into a global war between the East and the West, most of which would be fought on their continent.

Differences between Europe and the United States came to a crisis after President Truman announced that he would use whatever means were necessary to end the war in Korea. He refused to exclude atomic weapons.

Western Europe was shocked and outraged by Truman's statement. In Vienna, the story was the lead in all the newspapers, while in Rome, one paper even reported that the Tokyo bomber command was prepared to take off with an atomic bomb on a moment's notice. News commentator, Howard K. Smith referred to the European reaction as, "one of the most amazing political upheavals in Europe since the war." He reported from London that "British attitudes toward the United States had not been so testy for several years."

Similar reports of discontent were filed in other European capitals. Responding to the clamor in London and in other capitals of Western Europe, British Prime Minister Atlee flew to Washington seeking reassurance that the United States would not use atomic weapons or expand the war against China. His decision to go to Washington was widely hailed throughout Europe.

The simultaneous visit to London by French Prime Minister Rene Pleven was taken to mean that Atlee would represent all of Western Europe. The talks in Washington resolved some differences. Nonetheless, Atlee failed to gain the reassurances he wanted, especially with respect to China.

In the months that followed, Britain, the United States and most of Western Europe continued to disagree over the China policy. Eventually, with considerable diplomatic and political finesse, the United States was able to get through the United Nations a resolution condemning China as an aggressor nation. Even so, it did not have its way at the UN without causing a deep rift within the Western coalition.

All of America's Western allies objected to the U.S. position, maintaining that it would make it all the more difficult to negotiate with the Chinese and might even lead to Soviet involvement in the Korean conflict.

When Atlee continued to press the Americans on the question of Chinese membership in the United Nations, Truman and the Secretary of State, Acheson stuck firmly to their view that this question was not negotiable as long as China continued aggression in Korea.

During the winter of 1950-1951, a great debate took place in the United States. The debate was over whether the U.S. should make Europe or Asia its first line of defense. Senator Robert Taft of Ohio, the likely Republican candidate for President in 1952, as well as other Republican leaders spoke out against any large contingent of American soldiers going to Europe.

Europeans watched this debate with growing concern. They were fearful that the United States might abandon Europe in favor of Asia. The Europeans were even more alarmed at the possibility of a nuclear war between the U.S. and the Soviet Union, a war in which their citizens would be the first casualties. Seeking to resolve differences between the East and the West, they persisted in their protests against Washington's policy.

Also muddying relations between Washington and its European allies was the long-standing conviction that General MacArthur, whom the Europeans assailed for wanting to plunge the United States into a major Asiatic war, had undue influence in Washington. They were especially angered by MacArthur's action in turning what was intended to be a peace initiative from Washington into an ultimatum to the Chinese, either to surrender or face total destruction.

The pro American London *Economist* called it a piece of unmitigated "mischief." Britain's foreign secretary, Herbert Morrison even commented to Sir Oliver Franks, Britain's Ambassador in Washington: "He seems to want war with China. We do not. It is no exaggeration to say that by his public utterances, he has weakened public confidence in this country and in Western Europe in the quality of American political judgment and leadership."

Many Europeans believed that this episode reflected the whimsical and erratic nature of American foreign policy. It was with much relief, therefore, that Europe received the news of MacArthur's firing, following the release of a telegram that he had sent to House Minority Leader Joseph Martin criticizing the administration for fighting a limited war in Korea. In the House of Commons cheers went up at the news that MacArthur had been relieved of his duties.

Important papers in France such as *Le Monde, L 'Observateur, and Franc-Tireur* emphasized the great danger MacArthur might have created by bombing Manchuria. The firing of MacArthur narrowed the differences only marginally because Washington made it clear that it did not mean any change in U.S. policy in the Far East. It thus refused a request from London that Beijing be allowed to participate in a peace treaty and remained firmly opposed to giving the People's Republic of China a seat at the United Nations. Indeed, it increased pressure on the UN for harsh economic sanctions against China.

Following a successful UN offensive that once more drove the communists above the 38th parallel along most of the battlefront, the Chinese and North Koreans agreed to commence armistice negotiations with the United Nations. It soon became clear that an agreement would not come speedily or lead to Korean unification.

One of the main issues that prolonged the talks was the disposition of the prisoners of war (POWs.) Meanwhile, South Korea refused to sign any armistice that would keep Korea divided. The South's Syngman Rhee sought to press his view by releasing thousands of North Korean POWs who did not want to return home. The United States then arbitrarily decided Rhee could not be trusted. The CIA developed plans to remove him in a coup d'état. The coup was never completed. The British tended to blame American recalcitrance for the slow progress on this and other issues. They increasingly expressed their frustration at not having their own representative on the negotiating team.

Even the Conservative government of Prime Minister Winston Churchill, which was highly supportive of U.S. policy, felt that its voice was not heard in Washington.

The POW issue was finally settled in June 1953, the year the UN, North Korea and China signed an armistice agreement. The fighting ended. Significantly, South Korea refused to sign.

The Korean War was one of the most destructive of the 20th century. Four million Koreans died and two thirds of them were civilians. China lost up to one million soldiers. The U.S. suffered 36,934 dead and 11,949 wounded. The economic and social damage to the Korea Peninsula was incalculable. Three years of bombing left hardly a modern building standing. On the other hand, the Korean War was responsible for the establishing America's chain of military bases around the world and its enormous defense and intelligence system at home.

EUGENE H. VAN DEE

CHAPTER XIX

RWANDA

Rwanda, a Republic in east central Africa, is bounded on the north by Uganda, on the east by Tanzania, on the south by Burundi, and on the west by Lake Kivu and the Democratic Republic of the Congo. Kigali is its capital and largest city.

The Rwandan genocide, which claimed the lives of more than a million people in a three-and-one-half month period in 1994, was one of the greatest human rights disasters of our time. Nonetheless, the Clinton administration responded by downplaying the crisis and impeding effective intervention by U.N. forces to stop the killing. The reasons for its stance were bureaucratic inertia, American distrust of peacemaking in Africa, and general U.S. withdrawal from engagement in countries in which there was no strong domestic constituency.

Perhaps the most striking indication of the administration's approach to the crisis was that State Department officials refused to call the killing genocide until critical press articles forced Secretary of State Warren Christopher to finally invoke the term.

In 1992, the U.N. Security Council voted to deploy a contingent of peacekeeping personnel known as UNAMIR. At subsequent meetings, however, the United States urged complete withdrawal of the force on the grounds that it could not carry out its duties. As a result of this American pressure, the Council reduced the UNAMIR force to a skeleton crew of just 250 men. This decision, coming as it did at the height of the massacres, had enormous practical and psychological consequences inside Rwanda. It made it impossible for existing troops to expand their efforts to protect the tens of thousands of Tutsi and it sent an unmistakable signal to the genocidal forces that there would be no impediment to them finishing the job. The UNAMIR reduction was the single most important decision made with respect to Rwanda and U.S. policy choices thereafter largely derived from it.

The State Department's Africa Bureau argued fiercely in favor of a more vigorous UNAMIR presence in Rwanda. However, the Africa Bureau did not have the support of the higher-ups at State. The Undersecretary for Political Affairs, Peter Tarnoff, had no interest in Rwanda. The Undersecretary of State for Global Affairs, Tim Wirth, played no role at all in the question of U.S. policy during the genocide, although his brief included human rights. Moreover, Pentagon officials adamantly opposed an enhanced U.N. presence in Rwanda.

The disastrous American experience in Somalia was present at every discussion of Rwanda and was the most important factor in the military's opposition to international engagement elsewhere on the African continent. Thus, when the various agencies met on Rwanda, the Pentagon sent its top brass to make the case against a U.N. humanitarian intervention. The lack of consensus between the bureaus should have been resolved by Secretary of State Warren Christopher. Instead, it was the excuse for the Department's top tier to avoid the issue altogether.

With the entire region affected and the Rwandan Tutsi population at risk of total extermination, U.N. Secretary General Boutros-Ghali returned to the question of humanitarian intervention, asking the Security Council to cancel the reduction of the UNAMIR presence and to take "forceful action to restore order and end the massacres."

The United States refused to commit its own troops to the effort; thereby reducing the prestige of the mission and discouraging troop-contributing nations from participating. It also impeded the deployment by stalling on its commitment to provide equipment for the force. The lack of resolve by Washington to make the system work became a symbol of U.S. policy in general toward the disaster.

According to the State Department, the National Security Council, the Pentagon, and intelligence officials, the executive branch dithered endlessly. At no time did any senior figure in the Clinton White House or the State Department focus on the larger issue: the effect that foot-dragging and red tape were having on the ability of the United Nations to respond to the genocide.

With no public constituency urging American involvement and with no leadership in forming creative responses in Washington, Rwanda simply languished on the Democrat's watch.

Instead, it was the excuse for the Department's top tier to avoid the issue altogether. With the entire region affected and the Rwandan Tutsi population at risk of total extermination, U.N. Secretary General Boutros Boutros-Ghali returned to the question of humanitarian intervention, asking the Security Council to cancel the reduction of the UNAMIR presence and to take "forceful action to restore order and end the massacres". The United States refused to commit its own troops to the effort, thereby reducing the prestige of the mission and discouraging troop-contributing nations from participating. It also impeded the deployment by stalling on its commitment to provide equipment for the force. The lack of resolve by Washington to make the system work became a symbol of U.S. policy in general toward the disaster. According to State Department, National Security

Council, Pentagon, and intelligence officials, the executive branch dithered endlessly. At no time did any senior figure in the Clinton White House or State Department focus on the larger issue: the effect that footdragging and red tape were having on the ability of the United Nations to respond to the genocide.

With no public constituency urging American involvement and with no leadership in forming creative responses in Washington, Rwanda simply languished on the Democrat's watch.

CHAPTER XX

VIETNAM WAR

Fought from 1959 to 1975, the war pitted the North Vietnamese and the National Liberation Front (NLF) in conflict with United States forces and the South Vietnamese army. From 1946 until 1954, during the First Indochina War, the Vietnamese had struggled for independence from France.

At the end of that war, the country was temporarily divided into North and South Vietnam. North Vietnam came under control of the Vietnamese Communists who had opposed France and who aimed for a unified Vietnam under Communist rule. The South was controlled by Vietnamese who collaborated with the French.

The United States became involved in Vietnam because it believed that if all the country fell under Communist control, Communism would spread throughout Southeast Asia and beyond. This belief was known as the "domino theory."

The United States sent troops in 1965 to prevent the South Vietnamese government from collapsing. Ultimately, however, the United States failed to achieve its goal and in 1975, Vietnam was reunified under Communist government control, officially becoming a Socialist Republic. During the conflict approximately four million Vietnamese on both sides (South and North) were killed and more than 58,000 Americans lost their lives.

American intelligence in Vietnam was a bust. The CIA never penetrated the higher reaches of the enemy, nor did the Agency fully convey the weaknesses of the Saigon regime to Washington.

Historian Richard Helms, discussing the CIA in Vietnam, offered a stunning indictment: "We were dealing with a complicated cultural and ethic problem which we never came to understand. It was our ignorance which led us to miss assesses, not comprehend, and make a lot of wrong decisions."

Distressing indeed... the CIA, like the rest of the national security bureaucracy, bungled cluelessly during the most important conflict of the Cold War.

There will never be another year in America like 1968, one of the most tumultuous times in American history. It began on an ominous note when one of America's most fervent enemies, North Korea, seized a U.S. Navy intelligence ship, the Pueblo in the Sea of Japan. They held the ship and its crew captive for many months. In Vietnam, the massive Tet Offensive, launched by the Viet Cong caused enormous casualties on all sides.

The assassination of Dr. Martin Luther King touched off numerous riots in dozens of American cities. Senator Robert Kennedy, the brother of a murdered President, was assassinated in Los Angeles allegedly at the hands of an Arab fanatic. Colleges across the country were enveloped in a wave of protest and violence because of the Vietnam War, which was killing hundreds of young Americans every week.

In August, the Democratic Presidential Convention in Chicago was wrecked by thousands of young people who fought the Chicago police on live TV, symbolizing the anguish of a divided nation. Richard Nixon was elected President and man made his first tenuous step into eternity as Apollo 10 astronauts said, "Christmas prayers from the dark side of the moon." It seemed as if anything could happen that year.

And then, there was My Lai. The hamlets of Son My and My Lai were the scene of continued fighting. The entire area was covered with mines and booby traps taking a heavy toll both physically and psychologically on the American soldiers. On the night of March 1, 1968, the men and commanders of Charlie Company, which had been hardest hit by the traps, gathered outside of the "hooch" of the commanding officer Captain "Mad Dog" Medina who briefed the company on the next day's assault on My Lai. The men saw the next day's mission as an opportunity to pay back the Viet Cong for their booby traps, their mine fields and the blood of their comrades.

The men of Charlie Company began to assemble and nine Huey transport copters began to crank up their turbines. On board of one of these choppers was Army photographer Ron Haeberle, assigned to record the assault for Stars and Stripes, the Army newspaper. Less than fifteen miles away, the people of My Lai slept unafraid, unsuspecting; their dreams filled with visions of a peaceful future, unaware of the sword of vengeance that was about to fall on them; a nightmare for which nothing could have prepared them.

Other gunship appeared near the edge of My Lai and artillery preparation of the landing zone began. By this time, the residents of the village became aware of the impending attack. Even though no enemy personnel had been observed from the air, U.S. gunship descended on the scene and laid down a terrifying barrage of rockets and M-60 machine gun fire. Meanwhile, the 1st Platoon commanded by Lt. Calley moved into My Lai.

The first killing was an old man in a field who shouted a greeting in Vietnamese and waved his arms in friendship. Soldiers opened up on the Vietnamese farmers as they moved throughout the village. They fired at anything that moved.

Cows, pigs, chicken, water buffalo, and birds were blown apart by machine gun fire and M-79 grenade launchers.

The platoon advanced further into My Lai without receiving any enemy fire at all. As the villagers attempted to flee, they were pushed back inside the straw huts into which soldiers tossed grenades. Inside the village Vietnamese of all ages were rounded up in groups, then shot. Women and children, even babies were killed in their homes. Many young girls were raped while their families were forced to watch. Captain Brian Livingston, helicopter pilot, wrote in a letter back home on that very day: "I've never seen so many people dead in one spot. Ninety five percent were women and children."

Charlie Company had not received even one round of enemy fire. However, the entire hamlet of My Lai had been completely destroyed. The dimensions of the slaughter were so enormous, that the exact number of dead could not be accurately established. The official memorial in the village of My Lai lists 504 killed: 182 women of whom 17 were pregnant. 173 children of whom 56 were of infant age. Sixty of the men killed were over 60-years-old.

The *New York Journal* of September 16, 1965 printed a story stating: "There is a new breed of Americans, the 18 and 19 year-olds who have steel in their backbones and too much of what prize fighters call the killer instinct. These kids enjoy killing Viet Kong...No attempt is made to discriminate between military and civilian targets.U.S. planes rain death with 1,000-pound bombs, napalm and white phosphorous killing Viet Kong guerillas, innocent peasants, women and children."

The My Lai cover up continued for months and into 1969. Lies were told, false reports were filed by U.S. personnel. Only one man had proof of what happened on

March 16, 1968. Only one man had the refutable evidence of the killing and the incredible brutality at My Lai. That man was Ron Haeberle, the army photographer who witnessed the bloodbath. His shocking photographs of the carnage would shame a nation and break the heart of America.

In 1965, the American public first learned that U.S. planes were engaged in chemical warfare, deliberately using defoliants and herbicides to destroy rice and other crops in South Vietnam. A *New York Times* dispatch reported that up to 75,000 crop-producing acres had been sprayed.

Another *Times* story, in July 1966, noted that the spraying was being stepped up, blighting over 130,000 acres of rice and other food plants. As part of Operation Ranchhand, the U.S. dropped millions of gallons of chemical plant killers, such as Agent Orange, to destroy trees and foliage that provided the enemy cover. Racial prejudice was evident in the cruel and brutal character of this U.S. war of conquest, illustrated by the use of torture and the killing of prisoners.

In using herbicides, the United States was violating international norms against resorting to chemical weapons in war. Later, Agent Orange was found to cause birth defects and various forms of cancer to which many hundreds of American Vietnam veterans fell victim.

How did the United States get so involved in a war so far removed from its direct national interests? A war that took a toll of over 47,000 battle deaths and 10,000 other deaths and cost over $100 billion, all with totally negative results? It came about gradually, and it came about partly because of the persistent and erroneous view of American leaders that communism comprised a vast, well coordinated monolith that threatened to dominate the world. When the Americans slid into Vietnam, they knew it would be difficult, for they knew what had happened to the French before them. Still, it should not be assumed that the French were simply pushed out. Much is made of the French loss at Dien Bien Phu but their defeat there did not mean that the whole country had been forfeited. The French simply concluded that the cost was not worth it. They wisely decided to pull out altogether. American involvement began merely as aid to the French. Then as economic and military aid to the South Vietnamese.

Finally, The Gulf of Tonkin Resolution in 1964 amounted to a congressional declaration of war, and American military intervention began on a large scale. American troop strength rose to 27,000 by March 1965, to 74,000 by June, to 156,000 by the end of 1965 and reached the maximum of 541,000 in March 1969.

Aside from the absence of any positive results in Vietnam itself, the depletion of forces and material there for a decade represented a drain on resources that might have been used to bolster NATO and other allies and to relieve some of the economic stress at home. What made the intervention in Vietnam a real mistake was the American withdrawal ordered by President Nixon, handled in a disastrous manner, which practically guaranteed failure as far as South Vietnam was concerned.

During his campaign for the presidency, Nixon announced that he had a 'secret plan' to end the war. After he became President he ordered the withdrawal of 25,000 troops, to be followed by more. At the same time, Nixon stepped up the Phoenix Program, a CIA operation that resulted in the assassination of 20,000 suspected guerillas, most of whom were, in fact, innocent civilians.

The Cease-fire of 1973 meant nothing. The Americans pulled out altogether with no promise of any further aid. Two years later, the North Vietnamese overran the whole of South Vietnam, consolidating it into their realm. 165,000

South Vietnamese refugees fled to the United States and thousands more to other countries to escape the fate of their brethren that remained in their homeland. The withdrawal of American forces by unilateral decision invited the depredations against the local population.

On April 30, 1975, a CH-46 Marine helicopter lifted off the roof of The American embassy in Saigon. The last of the Americans were taken to safety aboard the USS Okinawa. It was not a proud day to be an American as the full extent of the betrayal struck home. We had given our solemn promise to the four hundred and twenty evacuees below not to abandon them. They had trusted America to the very end and then were shamefully left behind to be executed by the North Vietnamese. Things would have gone better for those people had there never been American assistance to stiffen their resistance, had there been no American military forces to promise protection.

This was another case of compounding one great mistake—the military intervention in the first place—with another—the unilateral withdrawal. Vietnam is not going to disappear. It is embedded in our moral history. We will always have to remind ourselves that we, a great and democratic nation, had been capable of monstrous deeds.

EUGENE H. VAN DEE

CHAPTER XXI

IRAQ

The Republic of Iraq is a country in southwestern Asia. The modern state of Iraq was created in 1920 by the British. Potentially, it is one of the richest countries in the world, with enormous deposits of petroleum and natural gas. Set up as a monarchy, Iraq became a Republic in 1958. Then it became a dictatorship dominated by a single party since 1968.

The dictatorship has been under the ruthless control of Saddam Hussein since 1979. It failed in various attempts to topple other Arab regimes and to achieve leadership status in the Arab world. It conquered Kuwait in 1990 but was forced to relinquish it by a coalition of Western and Arab countries in the Persian Gulf War. Afterward, it found itself shackled by an international oil embargo and other limitations on its sovereignty.

On September 20, 2002, George W. Bush told Congress that under his Presidency the United States could and would attack nations of his selection although they are not about to attack us. Since that day, the issue dwarfing all others in importance was whether the United States should wage wars of aggression. When on Bush's orders the U.S. military began bombing Iraq and then invaded it, the United States did in fact commit an aggressive war in violation of the United Nations Charter which says... "All members shall refrain... from the threat or use of force against the territorial integrity or political independence of any state."

Under Article 51 of that Charter, attacking in self defense is justified only "if an armed attack occurs" against a nation.

Iraq had not attacked the United States and contrary to the widely spread lie, there is absolutely no evidence that Saddam Hussein supported Al Quaeda or the 9/11 attack, or had any weapons of mass destruction. While the U.S. troops bombed and then conquered Iraq, the major television networks never focused on whether the United States should wage a premeditated war of aggression. They merely called American troops 'liberators.'

The Washington Post crusaded for this criminal war. Additionally, the *Wall Street Journal*, in its jingoistic ecstasy about attacking Iraq, all but posted a list of traitors who opposed it.

'Does the American president really have the power to make war at his pleasure?' is seldom asked by American press. They seem to be playing on the administration's team. 'Should President Bush have been allowed to conjure up and declare an aggressive war as national policy and then in speech after speech use Hussein's villainy to shove America into an illegal and murderous war against a nation one-twelfth its size?' 'How could a free and democratic people consent to America's young people and its weapons being used to attack a nation that neither attacked the United States nor was poised to do so?'

The reasons these questions go unanswered and even unasked include citizen and media ignorance of international law, more cowardice than courage among the people, and in the Congress and their knee-jerk nationalism. The transformation of the United States into a nation waging an aggressive war and further contemplates launching new wars on Iran, Syria, and North Korea, forewarns that American democracy may be in mortal peril... and America's allies? One only had to watch Collin Powell's face at the UN Security Council as Dominique de Villepin, the French

Foreign Minister, brilliantly expounded on peace and international ideals to know just how exasperating France can appear to ignorant outsiders. It made Powell angry and the British foreign minister turn a shade grayer. On the other hand, Villepin's lofty reasoning against war on Iraq drew applause from UN diplomats.

France's President Jacques Chirac has been at, or near, the top of the French government since long before George W. Bush re-found God. As Mayor of Paris, recurring Prime Minister or President, he has been busying himself with his country's destiny for close to forty years.

Still, why had France become so hugely involved? American official opinion points straight to oil. Iraq has the world's second largest reserves of petroleum. Hence, it makes sense that the U.S. should want a war in order to take control of Iraqi oil; while France rejected war, Americans say, in order to profit from options her oil companies hold to develop roughly twenty-five per cent of the Iraqi reserve.

However, if we look behind France's Security Council tussle with America, we would find the French conviction that the settlement of the Israeli-Palestinian conflict is the real priority in the Middle East, not the crushing of Iraq. France and Britain concurred, though Tony Blair could hardly wish to say so out loud. Courtesy of George W. Bush, he had put himself in a squeeze that threatened his very office.

Gerhard Schroder of Germany was on stage well before France or Britain. He said "no" to American plans for war. President Chirac took the lead from the German Chancellor and talked Russia into backing Germany and France. The trio gathered more support in the Security Council than America and Britain together could muster. Both men pushed George Bush to take the United Nations route rather than to make unilateral war on Saddam Hussein. President Chirac's watchword was: "there is an alternative to war…war is always an admission of failure." France believed that the Bush preventive war violated international law. "Let's not ignore western principles to crush Iraq. To do so, invites inter-national anarchy." Remembering only too well, the post World War II history of Algerian independence, the crucial case of Indochina, the full scale war between the French colonial regime and Ho Chi Minh's Democratic Republic of Vietnam, which marked the start of seventeen years of colonial war for France, climaxing in the downfall of the Fourth Republic in 1958, President Chirac, repeatedly stressed to George Bush the dangers to America of being caught in the Middle East quagmire. Bush refused to listen. He should have welcomed this French spanner being thrown into his war works, meant by the French leader to head off a potential clash of civilizations—Christian against Muslim— and thus, stifle terrorism.

To France, the war against terrorism is of vital importance. America's objectives are France's objectives too. France proved it by helping the U.S. achieve them. After the 9/11 attack on New York, the French press declared: "we are all Americans."

A significant part of the French fleet, including the flagship carrier Charles de Gaulle, was deployed in the Arabian Sea. French ground and air forces were in action from the beginning and played their role in the Security Assistance force in Kabul, as well as with Americans fighting al-Qa'ida.

The French have cooperated actively in the coordination of measures to improve the allied capacity to deal with the increasingly subtle cross border activities of international terrorism, and to identify and confiscate its financial assets.

Americans might also wish to remember that President Chirac was the first foreign leader to visit the site of the US September 11 bombing of New York. Can there be a more direct and sincere token of friendship?

Let us look back into history. When Charles Lord Cornwallis realized he had been beaten at Yorktown, Virginia, on October 19, 1781, he ordered his second in command to deliver his sword to Comte de Rochambeau, the French general who had supported General George Washington in the crushing defeat of the British thanks to a powerful naval blockade by the French fleet. In their schoolbooks, American children learn how France came to the assistance of the United States when all was at risk.

When General John Pershing, head of the American Forces, stepped onto French soil in 1917, he famously declared: "Lafayette, we are here." And yet, since the end of World War II, the United States and France have suffered a disaffection. To hear the anti-French invectives in the U.S. media since Bush's invasion of Iraq, one would never know that they were bound by a shared heritage bought with blood.

The depth of anger with the French is truly appalling. Internet communities and politicians are awash with anti-French jokes expressing contempt, hurt and incomprehension. This is the type of thing that gives the French 'les boules,' an expression signifying that they are choking with rage. "This is no longer a rational issue, its an emotional question," holds Dominique Moisi, head of the leading French think tank, the Institut Francais des Relations Internationales. This is a rejection of war and a rejection of America because war itself is the biggest evil." The French president had been saying the same thing, while outraged Americans accused him of appeasement.

EUGENE H. VAN DEE

CHAPTER XXII

KGB

Yes, the *Komitet Gosudarstvennoy Besopasnosti* (KGB) was declared officially dead on October 24, 1991. Almost immediately it was immediately reborn like the legendary Phoenix rising from the ashes, and divided into different parts that each quickly began a life of their own. The KGB was never a faceless, monolithic, omniscient, omnipotent operation but it always did and still does have highly skilled people with exemplary capabilities.

The labyrinth that is the Agency's history starts with CHEKA, which lasted from 1917 to 1922 and then continued with GPU (State Political Directorate.) GPU functioned in 1922 and 1923, and then became the OGPU (United States Political Directorate) lasting from 1923 to 1934.

The most ruthless secret police force operated from 1934 to 1946 -the years of Stalin' mass purges before and after World War II -under the initials NKVD (People's Commissariat of Internal Affairs.)

Later still, all security matters were merged into the MVD, the Ministry of Internal Affairs, under Lavrenti Beria, Stalin's notorious secret police chief.

From 1954 on, the KGB went through a series of internal changes, expanding and contracting, constantly involved in Soviet leadership's positions on domestic and international issues and events. From the ebullient heavy-handedness of Nikita Krushchev to the corrupt bonhomie of Leonid Brezhnev, the KGB maintained its influential role and organizational solidity. Together with the leadership of the

Communist Party and the armed forces, the KGB was regarded as one of the three major pillars of the state structure. Amoeba-like, the KGB split into several parts but the most important function was its ability to maintain the continuity of its international espionage operations. In 1992, what used to be the KGB's legendary First Chief Directorate became an independent spin-off-Russia's Foreign Intelligence Service (FIS.)

Throughout the years of the Gorbachev regime, the question on everyone's mind was whether the KGB could really be "reformed" or were its clandestine habits so ingrained that it would retain, no matter what its public protestations, its tactics of extralegal surveillance, communications' interception, infiltration of institutions, disinformation and manipulation at home and abroad.

Yevgeniya Albats, news analyst for the *Moscow News* wrote in 1992 that the KGB underwent merely a facelift, after which it rapidly consolidated its position. While the signs on doors were altered and department heads removed, nothing fundamentally changed. One shake up followed another. There were conflicting signals from competing authorities, innumerable rules handed down to KGB's foreign residents, plus wave after wave of revelations and denials, scandals uncovered and scandals covered up. The truth of the matter is that within the various KGB spin-offs, people didn't really know themselves what was going to happen next, or who, and what policy, would come out on top.

On the last annual State Security Workers Day in Russia, President Vladimir Putin gave a nationally televised address celebrating the 82nd anniversary of the CHEKA, the Bolshevik secret police that preceded the KGB. Putin's salute to the CHEKA was an image-builder, casting the security and intelligence services in heroic terms. Then he hosted a gala at the Lubyanka, the Moscow headquarters of the former KGB, to pay homage to CHEKA founder Feliks Dzerzhinsky. The CHEKA was reorganized as the GPU in 1922, later the OGPU, whose functions were transferred to the NKVD (Peoples Commissariat for Internal Affairs.)

When Lavrenti Beria was appointed head of NKVD, the vast apparatus of the Soviet security organs became the most powerful and the most feared section of society. In 1946, the NKVD became the MVD (Ministry of Interior.) After Stalin's death Beria was arrested on charges of conspiracy and executed. After Beria's fall, the security services were placed under the KGB (Committee of State Security.)

Under Gorbachev's policies, the power of the KGB was greatly curtailed. It was restricted to counter intelligence while foreign intelligence was assigned to the new Central Intelligence Service. With the collapse of the Soviet Union, Russia absorbed the KGB's remnants, combining most of them under the Security and Internal Affairs Ministry.

President Boris Yeltsin ordered the ministry replaced with a new Federal Counter-intelligence Service (FSK) in 1993. This arrangement baffled some observers who recalled that Yeltsin himself had earlier been a target of the KGB. Yet, like other leaders of ex-Soviet republics, Yeltsin felt the need for a secret service as long as he could be fairly sure of its loyalty to his administration.

The latest acronyms are a historic continuation of earlier reorganizations, from CHEKA to MVD. Ideologies fade and national identities tend to sharpen. Russia itself remains a great power relentlessly engaged in an intelligence renaissance. The KGB by any other name will still be the KGB. That old self-created air of omniscience, of faceless danger, of power beyond control will surround the Russian and other ex-Soviet secret services for decades to come.

EUGENE H. VAN DEE

SOURCES

National Security Archive
Arms Control Act
Questia Online Library
British Library
Freedom of Information Act
Agaf ha-Modi'in, Tel Aviv
Archive de l'armée de la Terre, Paris
2eme Bureau, Paris
Archive du Ministère des Affairs Étrangères, Paris
The Tricheco Files, VS 3&9, The Vatican
Delevov Petersburg
Komsomolskaya Pravda

BIBLIOGRAPHY

KGB: Masters of the Soviet Union, by Deriabin, Hippocrene Bks. NY 1990

Inside the KGB, by Kizichkin, Pantheon Bks, New York. 1990

The KGB: The eues of Russia, by Rositzke, Doubleday, NY 1981

The KGB: Death and Rebirth, by Ebon, Praeger, CT, 1994

Mutual Contempt: Lyndon Johnson-Robert Kennedy, by Meagher, 1999 Russia's political Tool, by Russian Information Services, 1997 Vladimir Putin and his predecessors, by Gaddy, The National Interest, 2002

The American Heritage Book of Indians, by Brandon, Heritage Pubs., NY 1961

The 15 Great Mistakes of the Cold War, by J. Huston, World Affairs, 1987

Texas and the Mexican War, by Stephenson, Yale Univ. Press, 1921 Guide to Indian Wars, by McDermott, Univ. Nebraska, 1998

Reflections on the Cuban Missile Crisis, by Garthoff, Brookings Institution, 1987

Cuba: The United States and Batista, by Thomas, World Affairs, 1987

Cuba: Anatomy of a Revolution, by Huberman, Monthly Review, 1961 Eavesdroppings: From the Bay of Pigs to Iran-Contra, by Wines, Washington Monthly, 1992

HaFilosofia shel HaModi'in, by Yitzak ben Yisrael, Ministry of Defense, Israel, 1999

The Battle for Guatemala, by S. Jonas, Westview Press, 1991

Cultures of United States Imperialism, by Pease, Duke Univ. 1927 The U.S. in Central America, by T.D. Schoonover, Duke Univ. 1993 Vietnam: Revolution in Transition, by Duiker, Westview Press, 1995 Fidel Castro, by R. Quirk, Norton NY 1993

Chile and its Relations with the U.S., by Evans, Duke Univ. 1927 The Art of the Coup, by Doyle, NACLA Report, 1997

Morning Glory, Evening Shadow, by Chang, Stanford Univ. 1997

Death in Life, by Lifton, Random House, 1968

Revolution and Counterrevolution, by Walker, Westview Press, 1991

The Greatest Threat: Iraq, by Richard Butler, Public Affairs, 2000

Secret Empire: The KGB in Russia, By Waller, Westview Press, 1994

Korea and the World, by Young Whan Kihl, Westview Press, 1994

The Southern Philippines, by Smith, New Zealand Review, 2002

Learning from Somalia, by Clarke, Westview Press, 1997

The Century of U.S. capitalism in Latin America, by O'Brien, Univ. of New Mexico, 1999

The Rise and fall of the American Army, by Stanton, Presidio 1985

Crisis Diplomacy, by Graber, Public Affairs Press, 1959

South America and the world Economy, MacMillan Press, London 1983

INDEX

Santa Anna	Custer
Taylor	Magellan
Kearney	Cleveland
Doniphan	Parrot
Bush	Roosevelt
Mejia	Smith
Trist	Mella
Cherokee	Roa
Creek	Rodriguez
Seminole	Marx
Fox	Amado
Bad Axe	Maugham
Jackson	Balzac
Neruda	Gorky
Fuentes	Kant
Paine	Plutarch
Marcos	Maurois
Hearst	Darwin
McKinley	Gramsci
Liliuokalani	Davidkov
Aguinaldo	Gilpatric
Wood	Dobrynin
Welles	Bundy
Luciano	Rusk
Genovese	Adenauer
Dalitz	Bruce
Salisbury	Perle
Luther	Hussein
Althus	Gravier
Guevara	Burgoyne
Edwards	Talleyrand
Fitzgerald	Thorneycroft
Wayne	Rostov

Armas	France
Azurdia	Cronin
Torricelli	Freud
Wisner	Einstein
Helms	Munthe
Allende	Fanón
Vanderbilt	Kruschev
Stimpson	Grechko
Zelaya	Lansdale
Debayle	Sorensende
Chamorro	Gaulle
Schultz	Macmillan
Casey	Finletter
McFarlane	Chaban-Delmas
Tower	Lafayette
Ho Chi Minh	Chirac
Kissinger	Beaumarchais
Harmar	Mirabeau
Powhatan	Franklin
Berkeley	Ball
St. Clair	Arbenz
Jackson	Ydigoras
Miles	Cerezo
Apache	Doyle
Cheyenne	Dulles
Kiowa	Jagan
Shoshone	Walker
Geronimo	Somoza
Chief Joseph	Moncada
Gaitán	Garcia
Hugo	Pastora
Dostoyevsky	Ortega
Turgenev	Weinberger

North
Poindexter
Lemnitzer
Pinochet
Lumumba
Massasoit
Wayne
Harmar
Harrison
Crook
Sioux
Comanche
Arapaho
Blackfoot
Nez Perce
Crazy Horse
Captain Jack
Red Cloud
Cherokee
Martin
Helms
Saigon
Pueblo
Medins
Calley
Viet Kong
Nixon
Iraq
Powell
Cornwallis
Pershing
GPU
Beria

Brezhnev
Yeltsin
Powers
Angleton
Golitsin
Garblet
Turner
Knoche
Waller
CIA
Church
Iraq
McLemore
DeWitt
Enola Gay
Stalin
Powers
Barre
Aidid
Korea
MacArthur
Mansergh
Atlee
Taft
Franks
Mangas Coloradas
Seminole
Rhee
Luther King
Viet Cong
My Lai
Haeberle
Livingston

Tonkin
Phoenix
Al Quaeda
de Villepin
Rochambeau
CHEKA
NKVD
Putin
Gorbachev
Cabot Lodge
Johnson
Penkovsky
Nosenko
Ames
Wilson
Wells

Shackley
KGB
Schlesinger
Secades
Warren
Leahy
Churchill
Dresden
Somalia
Perrot
Mogadishu
China
Acheson
K. Smith
Pleven
Morrison

E 183.7 .D44 2004
Dee, Eugene H. van.
Rapacious octopus